The
EARTH
KITCHEN

The
EARTH
KITCHEN

SHARON BRYANT

HARPERCOLLINS*PUBLISHERS*

HEARTFELT THANKS TO J.C.M.

Library of Congress Cataloging-in-Publication Data

Bryant, Sharon (Sharon Haanes), date.

The earth kitchen / Sharon Bryant.

p.   cm.

Summary: In 1963, twelve-year-old Gwen tries to find the path
to recovery in a mental ward.

ISBN 0-06-029605-4 — ISBN 0-06-029606-2 (lib. bdg.)

[1. Mentally ill—Fiction.] I. Title.

PZ7.B842 Ear 2002   2001024357

[Fic]—dc21   CIP

                                                        AC

Typography by Hilary Zarycky

1 2 3 4 5 6 7 8 9 10

First Edition

For my mother,
in loving memory

A safe fairy land is untrue to all worlds.
—J.R.R. TOLKIEN

The

EARTH
KITCHEN

CHAPTER ONE

Gwen loved the smell of crisp, clean sheets.

White sheets.

She pulled the hem of her white top sheet up over her head and pushed her small, bare feet against the rough cloth, making a tent. Bunching the white hem in her hands, Gwen brought the cloth to her nose and breathed in. It smelled of the *whoosh* of hot steam from the sheet press in the laundry as it pressed the wrinkled sail of cloth smooth and flat.

Some days, her favorite days, Gwen helped in the laundry, folding the warm pressed sheets. Girls were never allowed to work the sheet press, only to fold. And Gwen, along with whoever else was on folding that day, would make a dance of the job—hands out, hands together, come together, change—and the sheets would snap and bow.

Gwen would miss the laundry when she went home, the warmth, the *whoosh* of steam, the whiteness. It was good to think she'd miss something. Her toes rubbed against the taut crisscrossing of woven thread. Would it be the only thing? Gwen let go of the tented sheet. It billowed down onto her outstretched body, lost in the over-large nightgown that Aunt had sent for the warmer weather, sewn in a soft lawn with pink rosettes. The touch of the sheet coming to rest on her face felt cool and light as a breeze.

Gwen liked waking up before the other girls in the sleeping room, before the wake-up call to begin the activities of the day. Especially now that it was warm enough to have her window opened at night. Early morning sounds were like white sheets—simple, clean, single sounds that could be heard only when people were quiet. In the day here, they never were. And sometimes not at night either. But in the early morning hours, everyone was asleep, at least most of the time, and all Gwen had to do was listen.

A dog barked from a distance away, soft but sharp. Gwen liked it when dogs barked. She wished she had a dog, a little black one with silky hair and small black eyes, that she could bathe in the kitchen sink at home and take for walks on her own; she wiggled her toes at the thought of it. Gwen could feel the pressure of her folded quilt lying across the foot of the bed. None of the other girls had a quilt like hers, sewn all by hand. Just Gwen. She loved it best when it lay made up on her bed, smoothed over the pressed white sheets.

A breeze from the window blew a soft *swish* through the screen. Gwen reached down and pulled her quilt up over the top sheet. In the growing light, she could trace the patterns made by the cloth squares scattered across the quilt top in a patchwork of lights and darks. Scraps of this and that, Aunt had said. Scraps of peach-colored print from one of Aunt's aprons, scraps of robin's-egg blue from a dress made for someone grown and gone from the family long before Gwen had come. Scraps of Gwen's memories as she and Aunt had pulled the soft cut squares from a basket and pieced them together with needle and thread.

Gwen enjoyed sewing the squares, loved watching Aunt, a big hoop in her lap, making the tiny stitches to hold the layers of the quilt together. After the long months away, the rows of stitches seemed to march through her quilt like minutes; stitches like minutes, lined up in a row to hold together hours and days and months.

How many minutes had she been away? Many, many minutes. Too many to count, probably.

A car passed along the road, in through her thoughts, and out the other end. People said that a car engine purred. Gwen supposed that cars did purr, but a thrumming, urgent purr, not soft like the purr of a kitten. She wished she had a kitten, too, a calico kitten to sit on her

5

lap while she stitched squares, and to sleep on her pillow at night.

A sudden fluttering at the screen startled her. A moth? No, too loud for a moth, and no light for a moth to fly to anyway. Maybe a bird? Gwen longed for birds to come to her window, but they never did. It couldn't be a bird.

She had wanted, after coming here this past winter, to set out food for the birds on the broad stone sill outside the window by her bed, as she and Aunt had done outside the kitchen window at home. She had even asked if she might. She could have saved some bread from her dinner. But the whole idea had been impossible, if only she had thought it through, and for one obvious reason: All the windows on the ward, the sleeping rooms, the clothing room, the day room, the small activities room, were barred on the inside with a thick wire grating from the top of each tall window all the way down to the bottom.

Gwen had heard from Alice, her best friend on the ward, that all the windows in all the red-brick buildings of the Unity State Hospital were barred and locked. Alice said they needed to be, too, because patients at this hospital were lunatics and murderers who would throw themselves, or anyone else, out a window anytime they felt like it if the bars weren't there.

But that didn't seem right.

Gwen was a patient here, and she never felt like throwing anyone out of a window, especially not herself, and she didn't think Alice did, either. Alice said that if there was ever a fire, or an atom bomb attack, they would all burn to a crisp in their beds because they couldn't jump out of the windows, because of the bars. Gwen didn't like Alice saying things like that. And it didn't make any sense. Who would jump out of a third-story window to save her life? If there was a fire, Gwen reminded herself, she just had to run from her sleeping room to the stairwell door and down the stairs to the outside door. She was on an open ward. The doors on her ward were never locked, not like some of the wards she'd heard about here. Gwen was thankful, at least, for that.

And if there was an atom bomb attack? Gwen would follow the staff, just as they'd practiced, down the stairs and into the north tunnel, underground. There was even a metal sign above the tunnel doorway that read FALLOUT SHELTER, in yellow letters against a black band, in case you weren't sure which way to go. Above the letters on the sign, the fallout symbol was clearly visible: a black circle with three yellow triangles inside, their points meeting in the center of the circle like a windmill.

Mrs. West, the head nurse, said that down in the tunnels they would all be perfectly safe from an atom bomb attack. After the blast, Gwen imagined, the radioactive particles would fall out of the sky—there would be no buildings anymore—like crystals of shattered air glowing a faint blue; the windmill sign would blow the poison crystals far away from the tunnel entrance, so that she, and the others, would be safe. And she loved going into the windless tunnels, felt safe surrounded by the heavy whitewashed arches of brick overhead, the damp underground smell, and the row after row of barrels stacked on their sides lining the tunnel walls.

Stamped in yellow on the metal lid of each thick cardboard barrel was a circle, a triangle in the circle, and the capital letters "CD" inside the triangle. Mrs. West said that the "CD" stood for "Civil Defense," and that meant protection against attack for the people of the United States of America. Gwen wondered what special liquid or powder or protective clothing was stored in the barrels that could protect the people of the United States of America against an atom bomb attack. If she knew what it was, she could ask for some for herself, to keep with her all the time.

She had finally found the courage to ask a day nurse what was in the barrels.

"Water," the day nurse had replied.

"Water?"

How could cardboard barrels filled with water protect

the people of the United States of America? Was that why Aunt had taught her to put a fresh glass of water on the nightstand before she went to sleep, to keep her safe? But Aunt always said it was in case she got thirsty in the night. Gwen wasn't allowed a glass of water by the bed at night here. Glass wasn't allowed in the sleeping rooms. Someone might break the glass and cut herself, or cut someone else.

Alice said that nothing could protect a person from an atom bomb attack because atom bombs were so powerful they could blow up a whole country in an instant. Then she would snap her fingers and say it would happen just like that, just like the snap of her fingers.

A renewed fluttering from the direction of the open window dispersed the dust of Gwen's thoughts like the shake of a rag. She turned her head to listen. It was probably a June bug, a disgusting June bug. She'd seen one a few weeks ago, in the last week of May. The ugly thing couldn't even get the month right! Its big copper-domed back had shimmered with a frantic action of wings and legs, buzzing and grabbing at the screen.

She might as well have a look. Gwen quietly rose to her knees and leaned from her bed to look out the window. Flying up against the screen was a small bird.

Its wings were raised like an angel's wings, brushing

again and again against the screen. Its eyes seemed to look right into hers, like black beads, opaque and shiny. Its head listed oddly to one side, and its beak was strangely shaped.

No. Not its beak. Something in its beak.

Gwen couldn't turn on a lamp by her bed to see the bird more clearly because there wasn't one. Bedside lamps were forbidden in the sleeping room; a girl might break the lightbulb in her hand and cut herself, or get an electric shock. Or she might burn the tips of her fingers touching the glowing glass.

Besides, turning on the lamp might startle the bird away, or wake someone.

Now the bird was flitting from side to side along the width of the screen. Every time its head turned toward the lightening sky, Gwen could almost see what it held in its beak: a small, misshapen piece of metal on a chain. It gleamed yellow, in spite of the dim light, like gold.

Gwen pressed her face into the wire grating in front of the open window, hoping to get nearer to the bird. But she could get her face only so close, and not near enough to touch the screen.

"What do you have in your beak, little bird?" she whispered through the grating.

At the sound of Gwen's voice, the bird stopped fluttering. It seemed to hang in the air in front of her like an ornament on a thread. She couldn't pull her eyes away from whatever the small bird had in its beak.

Then the bird let go of the object.

It fell slowly down Gwen's line of sight, too slowly, it seemed, for real time, down and out of sight below the stone sill to the ground three stories below. She heard it land with a rustle of leaves in the border garden of newly planted impatiens.

The bird perched, now, with its tiny claws on the stone sill, stretching its neck up and down as if it were having a good look at her. The light was growing so that she could see the bird more clearly: a cherry-colored breast, brown-and-white-streaked wing feathers, and black bead eyes.

Then all in an instant, the cherry-breasted bird flew away.

Gwen leapt from the metal grating at the window to the chair at the foot of her bed. She pushed her feet into her slippers and her arms into her summer robe. How could she even think of sneaking off the ward at night? It wasn't officially morning until the wake-up call. She must be crazy! She was going home soon. They were going to allow her to go home to Aunt.

Well, she hoped so.

She could ruin everything by doing this, ruin her

going home to Aunt, her moving back to her own bedroom with her very own bed and nightstand and chest of drawers. In her mind, Gwen saw her bedside lamp, the bumpy milk-glass base sitting on a crocheted square, its rosebud shade clipped with two loops of wire onto the glowing yellow-lit bulb.

But she had to go and find whatever the bird had dropped for her from its beak. This would be her only chance. The garden group had been planting the borders below the girls' sleeping room yesterday. They might work there again today. Anyone might find it, anyone but Gwen. She could ask to be shifted to the garden group, but Mrs. West would never change her. Nothing changed here because you wanted it to. Gwen had to go and find what the bird had brought for her.

And she had to do it now.

CHAPTER TWO

Gwen walked as quietly as she could along the row of beds that made up the girls' sleeping room. The women patients slept in smaller rooms, two or three to a room. But the girls were put in the one long sleeping room, all eight of them together, at the far end of the ward. Gwen's bed was midway down after Ellen's and Ann's and Beth's. In the beds between hers and the door there was Alice, who was snoring as usual, then Lynn, and Mary, and the new girl, Janet.

Janet had kept Gwen awake for three nights with her crying. Last night—thankfully—she'd been quiet. Gwen would have to be extra careful. If Janet woke up, she might start crying again, and then the night nurse would come.

There wasn't any getting away from people here. If a girl cried all night, then everyone else in the sleeping room had to listen to her or sleep through the noise if they could. Gwen envied Alice this one point; she could sleep through anything.

The beds were close together in the sleeping room, in a row along the window wall. Each girl's sleeping area was arranged exactly the same, with a cotton-tied mattress on a metal bed frame, a nightstand to the right, clothes-pegs on the far wall, and a straight-backed chair at the foot of the bed. There were no curtains between beds for privacy; curtains were not allowed. Some girls, when they first came here, were too shy to dress in front of the others. Gwen had felt shy, too, but she hadn't done anything as silly as dress under the bedcovers like some of the girls had done.

Well, not quite. On her first night, Gwen had pulled her long nightgown over her head and undressed under it like a tent, reversing the process the next morning. It was the only time she'd been glad that Aunt always made her new nightgowns too big, to give her extra room to grow. Now she was used to dressing in front of the other girls, used to having people all around her here, used to the routine.

"Gwen," a voice whispered from one of the beds. It was Mary. "Where are you going?"

"Shh! I'm going to the toilet. Go back to sleep."

Mary laid her head down.

A brand-new day and already a lie in it.

The lying bothered Gwen. From her first day here, she'd learned that if she told the doctors and nurses what she really thought or how she really felt, they scribbled on her chart and gave each other sideways looks.

And that always meant trouble.

Gwen remembered the day she had arrived, sitting with Aunt in the wood-paneled admissions room. Aunt's eyes had been wet, as if she might cry. She could see Aunt sitting there, wearing her navy-blue going-out hat with the grosgrain ribbon, her white hair wrapped underneath it like coiled rope. Why had Gwen answered the doctor's questions the way she did, insisting that Aunt write those things on the forms? That had started a lot of trouble for Gwen with the staff on the ward, who treated her as if she were crazy. Some of the women patients had teased her, too, though others told them to shut up, and couldn't they see she was just a little girl? Then someone would beckon to Gwen to come close, calling her "sweetheart" or "honey," and try to stroke her hand.

But lately, the women patients had forgotten all about her. And Alice had stopped any of the other girls from making jokes. Gwen, for her part, had learned not to say too much and to stay out of trouble.

Well, maybe.

What she was about to do right now didn't seem to show that she'd learned much at all. She felt like scolding herself for doing such a fool thing right before she might be going home. But in her mind, again, Gwen saw the cherry-breasted bird at her window, coming just to *her* window, with something for her in its beak.

Gwen reached the door that opened into the main hallway. It had a glass window in it like all the doors on the ward, except the toilet-room door. Embedded in the thick glass was a thin wire mesh, just like the chicken wire Aunt used to fence in the vegetable plot in the backyard at home, to keep the woodchucks from nibbling off the tips of the new peas. Same silvery color, too.

But how did they get the wire *into* the glass? It seemed impossible, wire into glass. She had asked a day nurse about it once, but the nurse had shrugged her shoulders, saying she didn't know, as if she didn't even care! Gwen peered through the cage of wire-embedded glass into the empty hallway and over to the nurses' station.

The two night nurses were sitting at their desks. One was reading a book; the other was talking on the phone. Soon they would be making their rounds to check the sleeping rooms. That might give Gwen a chance to get to the stairwell door, if they didn't come to check her sleeping room first.

But what if only one nurse at a time left the station? She could say she needed to use the toilet, but that wouldn't work. The night nurse would wait for her outside the toilet-room door and escort her back to bed. What she needed was something to distract them.

A scream pierced the quiet. It was coming from a sleeping room at the far end of the hall. The first nurse dropped her book and ran toward the scream. The second nurse, who was on the phone, hung up, dialed the phone again, spoke, hung up, and ran toward the scream too.

Gwen couldn't have planned anything as good as this! The night nurses were always running to quiet the screamers. Screamers woke up everyone on the ward if they were left to scream too long. Then it took a lot of work to settle everyone down. If Gwen were a night nurse, she'd run to a screamer, too, to save herself the extra work.

But the timing was perfect.

Whoever was screaming—and she'd be sure to find out later from Alice, who knew all the gossip on the ward—Gwen was going to give her a chunk of chocolate fudge from the package Aunt sent with her letter last week. She could slip it into the woman's cupboard in the clothing room, wrapped in a bit of wax paper so it wouldn't dry out.

Gwen pushed open the door to the sleeping room, ran the short distance to the stairwell door, opened it, and was through.

Gwen started down the stairs. She wasn't worried about running into the staff coming up to help the night nurses on the ward. Staff almost always used the staff-only elevator; the doors into the elevator were locked to patients. Of course, the girls were forbidden to go into the unlocked stairwells or walk from floor to floor unescorted by staff. Some of the girls had done it before in small groups, but never, to Gwen's knowledge, alone, or at night.

She hurried past the second floor, another ward for women that looked just like Gwen's ward. Sometimes the wards got together in one of the day rooms for a music night, with records and punch and popcorn. If it was just the women, the girls were always invited along. Some of the women even danced together to the music, shuffling from side to side with their hands on each other's waists, their cigarettes hanging like lit fuses from the corners of their mouths. But none of the girls ever danced. They just stood against the wall or sat in the shiny, padded day room chairs in their same old everyday clothes. Gwen never had much fun at the social events here. They always made her extra lonesome for home.

She passed the first floor, with the rec room, the large activities room, and the dining hall for all the wards in the Pineview Building, and headed down the stairs to the half-floor landing with the door that opened out to the grounds. Gwen had often been escorted this way to different activities outside Pineview when the weather was fine, and always to board the bus for outings away from the hospital.

Once, Miss Gordon, the activities therapist, and three of the day staff, took the girls to Kresge's Department Store for shopping and lunch. Some girls had purchases to make—a new shower cap, a comb, or a larger pair of shoes—but Gwen didn't need anything, so she and Alice just looked around. Everything had gone all right until lunchtime, when Lynn crawled onto the table of their booth at the Kresge's luncheonette to take a nap. Gwen grabbed her orange soda just in time. Forks and spoons clattered onto the seat. The ice water spilled. And Lynn's large, stained panties glared at everyone from under her scrunched-up skirt. When Miss Gordon came over to coax Lynn off the table, Lynn started cursing and kicking. One kick caught Miss Gordon right in the face, knocking her glasses to the floor. Finally, the staff got Lynn out of the luncheonette and out of the store. Gwen could hear her yelling and cursing in the parking lot. Everyone else could, too. So the girls had to finish in a hurry and rush out to the bus for the ride back to the hospital. Alice had laughed the whole way back. Gwen remembered wishing that Alice would just shut up.

If Gwen went another half flight down the stairs, she'd be in the basement area, where a door opened into the north tunnel connecting Pineview with all the other buildings of the hospital. Gwen had been escorted through the tunnels lots of times during the winter, and on stormy spring days, too, from the north tunnel to the service tunnel to get to her job at the laundry. And always down the stairs into the north tunnel when the air-raid horn sounded for a drill.

One afternoon, she walked all the way to the end of the north tunnel to visit with Aunt in the visitors' lounge in the Main Building. Aunt had made the long trip just to be with Gwen on her twelfth birthday, bringing her some new clothes for the warmer weather and a small cake that they ate picnic style on plates Aunt had brought from home. Gwen remembered not wanting to leave Aunt to go back to the ward, resisting the day nurse, pushing her away. But Aunt had said Gwen must go back with the nurse, that she should be a good girl and work hard to get well so she could come home soon, giving Gwen a long hug while she said it. Then the day nurse had said it was time, and Gwen let go of Aunt and walked with the nurse down the central corridor of the Main Building and into the north tunnel, toward Pineview, her birthday clothes in a paper sack tucked under her arm.

As she and the day nurse had walked back to the ward, Gwen remembered Alice saying that you could get anywhere through the tunnels, as long as no one stopped you. But to Gwen, the only important place was home with Aunt. She didn't think any of the tunnels would take her there.

Gwen had her hand on the metal bar of the outside door when she remembered the alarm. If she opened the door without a special key, an alarm would sound and someone would come searching for her right away. She looked up at the silvery metal box attached to the wall by the door. On the face of the box was a round keyhole, and above the keyhole, poking out from the shiny metal plate, was a small light, like a gumdrop, glowing red. It occurred to Gwen that the only really important possessions here were keys. The staff told her what to do and where to go because of the power they held in their rings full of keys. Keys gave a person power. And neither Gwen nor any of the other patients had a single key between them.

The door wasn't locked, just booby-trapped, and Gwen didn't have the key to stop the alarm from sounding. She could still go out. She had to go out and find what the bird had dropped for her in the border garden. But she'd have to run to get it before someone came to take her back inside. Later, she would accept whatever punishment was given her, the lecture from Mrs. West, restriction to the ward, meals in the small activities room for the next hundred years, and no talking to Alice.

But please don't let this stop her from going home.

Gwen held the metal bar on the door with one hand as she pulled a slipper off her foot with the other. She needed to stick something in the doorjamb to keep the door from locking shut on the outside after she went through. Maybe there was still a chance she could do this without getting caught, if she was quick.

Gwen pushed the door open, expecting a loud bell or horn, but there was no alarm, no sound at all. The light on the wall box glowed as steadily red as it had a moment before. She didn't hear the alarm, but someone had, and the silence unnerved her so that she fumbled the slipper right out of her hand. The heavy door slammed shut, leaving the slipper locked inside on the landing and Gwen, half barefoot on the concrete stoop, locked outside.

CHAPTER THREE

An outside light shining down on the concrete stoop made everywhere beyond its reach look dark and strange. Gwen remembered Alice saying that lunatics and murderers locked on the wards here would sometimes escape at night to roam the hospital grounds, looking for someone to kill. Why was Alice always saying things like that? What she said on the ward in the daytime seemed silly, even funny; but facing the darkness, Gwen wasn't so sure. What if Alice was right? What if a murderer or lunatic was waiting in the shadows, right this very second, to grab at her neck? Gwen felt a tightening around her throat.

But how could Alice know what happened here at night? She snored her head off all night long. And sometimes Alice said things about people that weren't exactly true. She just couldn't stop herself. Aunt always said that a person should judge not, lest he be judged. Gwen wondered if patients in the other wards thought that she and Alice were lunatics and murderers who roamed the hospital grounds at night looking for someone to kill. The idea of it! Even Aunt would laugh at that.

Then something else occurred to Gwen. Something she hadn't considered. What if there was an atom bomb attack right now? She wouldn't be able to get down to the tunnel because she'd locked herself out. Had anyone even noticed she was gone? Had the night nurses?

Gwen caught sight of her face reflected in the window of the outside door; her hair poked out like twig ends, and her shoulders crouched in the folds of her summer robe. She looked away, focusing on the brickwork above the top of the door. There was the black circle, the yellow triangles, and the words FALLOUT SHELTER. Gwen stared at the sign, her heart pounding in her chest. How would she get to safety without the key?

Her fist whipped into the air to hit at the door when a fluttering froze her arm, a swish of colored air between her fist and the door. A blur, and yet it wasn't a blur; she could see the cherry breast, the brown-and-white-streaked wing feathers flying in front of her fist to stop it. A wisp of movement, and yet she saw the bird clearly, its black bead eyes looking into her eyes. The bird had dropped something for her in the border garden below her sleeping-room window, was reminding her of it, the object she had come out to find.

Gwen dropped her arm and ran from the sheltering

tent of yellow light to the left, around the building, and along the border garden to the spot below the window by her bed. It was the spot where something had landed, with a rustle of leaves, dropped from the beak of the cherry-breasted bird. She had to find it, even if an atom bomb was falling toward her, aimed at the border garden below her window, on its way this very second.

Her eyes raced up the red-brick face of Pineview, counting three stories up, three windows from the corner. It should be right here.

Gwen fell to her knees in the damp earth, parting the leaves of the newly planted flowers with her fingers, patting the ground. The dirt felt moist and cool on her bare hands, soothing; her breathing steadied and her heartbeat slowed. What had she been so worried about? Her fingers sifted the soft dirt around the plump stems and saw-toothed leaves, taking care not to expose the tender roots.

But where was it? There was nothing here but plants and dirt.

She looked up, checking to see if she was in the right spot. She needed to move a little more to the left.

Here.

Gwen started searching around the plants in the new spot. She heard the *swish* of the outside door opening and the click of a flashlight being switched on. Her hands moved quickly through the leaves and dirt. In a few seconds she'd lose her chance.

Come on, come on. . . .

Got it!

The metal object, with its long chain, coiled in the palm of her hand. It felt heavy for its size and cool like the dirt in the garden. A necklace? Gwen shoved her hand into the pocket of her robe, letting the necklace slip into the sling of soft cloth. A flashlight beam progressed along the grass just beyond the corner of the building. Keys jingled. At least it wasn't a murderer or a lunatic; they wouldn't be allowed any keys. A man cleared his throat and spat. Gwen scrambled to her feet and stood next to the border garden.

The beam of light flashed in Gwen's eyes, blinding her. She raised a hand to cover her face as she heard the flashlight click off.

"What have we here?" It was Mr. Jones, the security guard. "Gwennie, is it? Up early and doing a bit of gardening, by the look of you. Well, they say the early bird catches the worm." He chuckled softly. "Just you then?"

Gwen nodded.

She looked down at her dirt-covered hands. On the front of her robe, two brown patches marked her knees. Gwen remembered her missing slipper and slowly tucked her bare, right foot underneath her robe and nightgown. It was against the rules to go barefoot, anywhere. They even had to wear flip-flops in the shower. Mrs. West said the rule was there to protect all of them against the spread of disease. Alice said it was because they were all contagious, and Mrs. West was afraid of catching *their* germs. Then she might land up as a patient in the hospital too. Gwen had laughed when Alice said that. No one came to this hospital because they'd caught a cold or the influenza. But later, she worried that she might be germy and unclean, a threat to other people, a threat to Aunt.

"You missing this, Cinderella?" Mr. Jones held out Gwen's lost slipper.

"Not *cinders*," Gwen said, firmly. She was uncomfortable with the thought of cinders and soot and fire. "It's dirt from the garden."

"Dirt, to be sure. Well, never mind it. A child has a right to a bit of fresh air on a fine June morning," Mr. Jones said. He cleared his throat. "Come on in, now. You can wash your hands and still have time for a bit of shut-eye before the drill sergeant sounds the wake-up call." He winked at Gwen.

Gwen took the slipper and pulled it onto her foot. She walked back to the door with Mr. Jones.

"Enjoy gardening, do you, Gwennie?"

Gwen nodded.

She usually didn't like being called Gwennie at the hospital, but it was all right coming from Mr. Jones. He was always nice to her and the other girls on the ward. And he asked the sort of questions that she could answer, not like most of the grown-ups here.

"They already know about this upstairs." Mr. Jones raised his eyebrows as if looking up to heaven. "But I'll see what I can do. Just getting a bit of fresh air and locked yourself out." He chuckled again. "Come on then, Gwennie, better be getting in."

They reached the door, and Mr. Jones unlocked it. Then they walked up the stairs. Gwen didn't dare put her hand into the pocket of her robe to touch the necklace. Better to wait. She mustn't risk anyone finding it and taking it away. The night staff would be preparing to go home soon, and the day staff would be coming in. With any luck, the day staff would deal with her after break-fast. Then she'd have some time to herself, before the others got up, to look at what she had found.

They reached the top of the landing. Gwen peered through the glass window into the ward. Everything seemed calm, in contrast to the screaming and rushing that had preceded her run to the stairwell. Outbursts seemed to build like that here, like silent puffs into a balloon, growing bigger and bigger, until suddenly the balloon would burst in a screaming fit, a grab at another patient, or a head knocking hard against the smooth plaster wall. Then, in the next instant, the burst balloon would collapse on itself, a harmless wad of rubber. And somewhere else a new balloon would begin building pressure all over again.

Gwen could feel the pressure building on the ward as she and Mr. Jones walked in. The night nurse was speaking to Mrs. West at the nurses' station. Mrs. West was still holding her coat and scarf; she must have just come in. In her starched white uniform with her white cap and stockings and shoes, she looked like a pillar of salt. Not that Mrs. West would ever break the rules, as Lot's wife did in the story. The head nurse *made* the rules. And everyone else had to follow them. Or accept whatever punishment they were given.

Mrs. West was looking down at her wristwatch; neither she nor the night nurse seemed pleased to see Gwen. The night nurse started toward them, but Mrs. West stopped her and walked over to Gwen and Mr. Jones herself.

"Gwendolyn, I am sure you have something to say for yourself, but it will have to wait until after breakfast. Please return to your sleeping room."

"Yes, ma'am." Gwen averted her eyes from the head nurse's stern gaze. It *would* have to be Mrs. West who was waiting at the nurses' station as she was brought in. Just Gwen's bad luck.

But what if this was going to keep her at the hospital the whole summer, keep her from going home to Aunt?

"Mrs. West?"

"Back to bed, Gwendolyn."

"I'll still be going home soon, won't I?"

"To bed, Gwendolyn. Now."

"But Mrs. West . . ."

"Not another word. To bed!"

"Yes, ma'am." Gwen turned and walked slowly to her sleeping room, hoping to hear what Mr. Jones was going to say.

"She just went out for a bit of fresh air," Mr. Jones said, chuckling.

"There is nothing amusing about running off the ward, Mr. Jones. Think of the danger."

"I know, I know. But she's back safe and sound with no harm done. That's all that matters."

Gwen looked back at both of them. Mrs. West was as stern as usual. Mr. Jones was smiling, trying to smooth things over. He looked over at Gwen and gave her a wink.

"And she spent her time useful-like, Mrs. West, doing a bit of gardening."

The head nurse's eyebrows leapt into sharp peaks. She noticed Gwen.

"To bed, *now!*"

Gwen rushed to her room, her hopes of going home to Aunt fading with every hurried step.

• • •

Of course, everyone was awake in the sleeping room, listening to what was going on out in the hall. Gwen walked to her bed. Some of the girls pretended to be asleep, but Gwen knew they were really awake.

"Psst! Gwen," Alice whispered from the next bed.

"Shh! You're going to get me into more trouble. Don't talk to me!" Alice could be so nosey.

"Shh, yourself!" Alice said, not even trying to whisper. She turned over in her bed and was quiet.

The light in the sleeping room was growing. Gwen was going to have to be careful. She slipped her hand into the pocket of her robe as she took it off, grasping the small necklace in her fist. Then she kicked her slippers toward the chair and jumped into bed, turning onto her side, away from Alice, who snooped into everything. Gwen pulled the covers over her head and brought her closed fist up to her eyes.

She opened it.

At first Gwen couldn't tell what she was looking at. The light was dim under the covers, with only the natural light coming in through the window. Her eyes adjusted, and suddenly she saw exactly what it was.

Nestled in the dirt-smeared palm of her hand was a coil of chain, and threaded onto the chain was a small gold key.

CHAPTER FOUR

A gold key!

At least it looked yellow like gold, felt heavy like gold, to Gwen. Hadn't she tried sewing with Aunt's gold thimble once, placing it on her middle finger to try to stitch the cloth squares together for her quilt? She couldn't work the thimble right, but Aunt had said it just took practice, that she would learn. And she had learned something about the feel of gold in her hand, about the smooth stippling at the working end of the thimble to catch and push the needle through, and the sharp swirl of minute leaves carved into the gold along the bottom edge. Gwen had remarked to Aunt about the weight of the thimble, so small to be so heavy, how the hard yellow metal looked as soft as butter.

"That's because it's pure gold, Gwennie, my love."

Pure gold.

Gwen traced the fine markings of the gold key with her finger. The key was small enough to fit in the palm of her hand. It had a round shaft and rampart teeth like the old keys Aunt kept in the green-enameled tin in the bottom of the storage cupboard, out in the summer kitchen. But those were dull gray tin keys, "retired," Aunt called them, and "hadn't they unlocked enough?"

On the top of Gwen's key, worked in the gold, were three leaves fanning out from the handle, two to one side and one to the other, coming together at their stems like a knot in a bow. They were oak leaves; Gwen was sure of it. She had a tree identification book at home, and there was a big oak tree in Aunt's front yard. Even the fine veins of the leaves were carved into the gold. And below the single leaf, in a cluster coming out from a twig, were three tiny acorns.

Gwen collected acorns. She usually looked for them in the yard and in the woods behind Aunt's house. When she found some, she would put them in her pockets, or even her socks, and take them home. Sometimes she would pry off the top of an acorn with a small knife and dig out the inside nut to make a secret acorn box, hiding a bead inside, or a tightly folded note, sticking the lid back on with modeling clay. Sometimes acorns even got into the wash! Aunt kept an old bowl on the laundry shelf just for acorns she found in Gwen's pockets or socks. Every once in a while, Gwen would find two acorns on one stem, but never three together like the acorns carved in miniature on her gold key.

Her gold key!

In the growing light it gleamed under the bedcovers like a golden promise. Gwen tucked her knees up and brought her arms around her legs as if she were hugging the gold key with her whole body. Her key didn't look like the hospital keys the staff carried around on huge metal rings. It didn't make that jangly sound, either. Her single gold key didn't make any sound at all. It wouldn't unlock the staff elevator, or stop the alarm from sounding when the outside door was opened, or release any of Alice's murderers or lunatics from their locked wards to roam the hospital grounds at night. It wasn't that sort of key.

Aunt kept the useful keys on a peg board by the back door at home. Each key hung on a short chain like a string of tiny silver pop beads, the two ends of the chain snapping into a candy-shaped clip to make up the loop. Gwen had often passed the time snapping the metal beads in and out of their little clips. The chain on her gold key was just like the chain on the keys at home, only longer, long enough to slip over her head.

But chains, necklaces, anything that went around a girl's neck, even wool scarves in the winter, were forbidden here, just in case a girl choked to death, or was made to choke by someone else. Gwen didn't like to think about things like that—unlike Alice, who was always talking about death. But what did she know about it? She had never been dead. Most of the girls tried to hide necklaces they secretly made from raffia or lacing from the craft room, or from lengths of frayed thread from a blanket or their own clothes. The nurses were always watching for that. Gwen let the pop-bead chain pour from the palm of one hand into the other. If she couldn't wear her gold key as a necklace, where was she going to put it to keep it safe?

It suddenly occurred to Gwen that one of the staff might try to take her key away, or another girl might steal it. Her hand clamped over her key. She had to hide it! Why hadn't she realized it sooner? Who on the staff would believe that the cherry-breasted bird had brought the key to her, brought the gold key especially for her, for Gwen, to keep? Who would believe that she was telling the truth, that she hadn't stolen it?

Alice would believe her. But Alice might tell someone else. She wasn't very good at keeping secrets. Then someone would report it to Mrs. West. No, she'd have to hide her gold key even from Alice, hide it before the day got under way, before she had to meet with Mrs. West for her punishment.

But where?

Gwen couldn't leave the key in her clothes cupboard. Nurses were always going through patients' things in the clothing room, and some girls looked into other girls' cupboards and took things when the nurses had their eyes turned away—Alice had seen them do it and told Gwen so. And if the staff noticed something in a girl's pocket, they did a pocket check. Gwen had lots of pockets in her dungarees, but not a secret one to keep something so special hidden. And her blouses didn't have any pockets. What about inside her sock?

A day nurse would be sure to see it through her thin white anklets, even if she unclipped the chain. Or it might fall out when she walked and become lost. Her sneakers fit too snugly, now, to hide her gold key and still have room for her foot.

Where was she going to hide it?

Gwen heard a click, and the sleeping room was suddenly bright.

"Good morning, girls."

It was Mrs. West.

"I expect all of you in line for the showers by the time I get back. Five minutes!"

Gwen had thought she would have more time to think. She needed more time! Through the bedcovers she could hear the other girls yawning and muttering, the sounds of the sleeping room making its shift from night to day. Alice groaned loudly in the bed next to hers.

"Hey, Gwen," she called over, "you heard her. Time to get up."

Something soft hit Gwen on the back. It was Alice's pillow. Alice always tossed her pillow at Gwen in the morning. It slid off the covers and onto the floor. Gwen knew what was coming next and tightened her grip on the top hem of her sheet. Hands grabbed at the bed-covers. "Leave me alone!" Gwen poked her head out from under the sheet and glared at Alice, who grinned down at Gwen like a scarecrow missing its stuffing, like pajamas hanging on sticks; she was *so* thin. Her hair stuck out every which way, like a fistful of straw.

"Heard you were sleepwalking last night," Alice said.

"You said you were going to the toilet," Mary mumbled, her eyes focused on the floor. "But you didn't come back for a long time. The nurse came in to check on us. She saw you were gone."

All the girls in the room stopped their preparations for the shower and looked at Gwen.

"Get into trouble, Gwen?" Lynn asked, too loudly.

Gwen pushed her key under her pillow and jumped out of bed. She didn't have to answer to any of them. It was none of their business. She'd just pretend this morning was like any other morning and come back for the key after her shower, when all the girls tidied up their sleeping areas. No one would think to look for her gold key before she got back. By then she might have figured out what to do.

Alice was making faces at Gwen, trying to get her attention. Gwen looked away. On the chair by the foot of her bed, she noticed a dirt-stained patch staring out from the folds of her summer robe.

"You sure are grumpy today," Alice said.

Sometimes Alice just couldn't get the message to mind her own business.

"Aren't you going to tell us what you were up to last night?" she continued. "Come on, Gwen."

All the girls gravitated toward Gwen's bed. No one was getting in line for the showers. Gwen reached for the top of her robe as Alice grabbed Gwen's pillow. Alice whipped the pillow up to toss it, baring the smooth white sheet underneath.

Gwen opened her mouth and screamed.

Her gold key was gone!

All the girls in the sleeping room started at the sound. Even Alice, still holding the pillow above her head, gaped at Gwen, her eyes wide as dinner plates.

"What in the world?"

Gwen bounded over the bed, grabbing Alice and pinning her down.

"You give it back, Alice, or I'll . . ."

Suddenly, there was Mrs. West.

"What is going on here? Gwendolyn, let go of Alice this instant."

Alice's thin arms tried to push Gwen away.

"Give it back!" Gwen shouted, staring hard at Alice. "It's mine, not yours. *Give it back.*"

"This seems to be your morning for disrupting the entire ward," Mrs. West said, pulling Gwen off Alice. Then, "All girls in line for showers, immediately!"

"Mrs. West, Alice took it from me. She didn't have the right. It's mine! I put it under my pillow to keep it safe. She stole my—"

"Enough, Gwendolyn. We will speak about this after breakfast. Girls, get in line! And I want silence. Now!"

They all did as they were told.

Gwen glared at Alice. She always ruined everything. The gold key was hers, brought to her by the cherry-breasted bird.

Her gold key.

The line began to move out through the door of the sleeping room toward the showers. Gwen shuffled along, her hands knotted in fists and her arms board straight against her sides.

As they passed the nurses' station, Mrs. West left the head of the line and nodded for a day nurse to continue with the girls. The head nurse walked over to a desk, dialed the telephone, and began to speak; she glanced up, her face set.

She was talking on the phone to someone about *Gwen*.

CHAPTER FIVE

Gwen sat on the edge of her neatly made bed. Her night-stand was tidied, and her hair was combed. It would be time to go down to breakfast soon, although she wasn't very hungry.

She had searched around her sleeping area, and grilled Alice, too, until she was satisfied that Alice hadn't taken her gold key, didn't even know what she was talking about. The key had simply disappeared.

The sleeping room door opened, and Mrs. West walked in.

"Everyone in line for breakfast!"

Mrs. West didn't look at Gwen.

The girls formed a line and followed the head nurse down the stairs toward the large dining hall. They reached the first-floor landing, and Mrs. West opened the door. The smell of coffee wisped into the stairwell as they walked through; it was even stronger in the hall. Gwen breathed it in. Aunt loved a cup of strong black coffee in the morning, no cream or sugar. It was the first smell

Gwen woke up to in the mornings at home. The smell of coffee *was* home, in a little way. It was a comfort to think of it now.

They walked through the double doors and into the large dining hall. Gwen covered her ears. It was so noisy in here! Utensils banged onto the food trays; everyone seemed to be talking at once; and the bonneted cafeteria staff shouted, "Good morning!" and "Move along!" to patients as they went through the serving line. It always took Gwen a few moments to get used to the noise of the dining hall. It seemed extra noisy today. She took her hands from her ears and picked up her tray.

Gwen walked over to the girls' table and slid onto the bench next to Alice. She set her breakfast tray down on the shiny table: real tabletop, real Alice trying to ignore her, real eggs and toast and juice. Doubt squeezed in next to Gwen on the bench. Maybe seeing the cherry-breasted bird at her window, sneaking outside to find the key, holding the gold key in her hand, maybe it hadn't really happened? Gwen pushed the thought away. She had found her gold key in the border garden. She wouldn't believe she had made it all up in her mind. She would not! Her breakfast was getting cold just sitting there on the tray. Gwen looked down at her lap and noticed dirt under the fingernails of her right hand. The corners of her mouth rose in a smile. She picked up a piece of toast and took a bite.

Gwen knew some of the girls made things up in their minds. Mary thought she'd killed her mother. But her mother came to visit her every Sunday.

Then there was Alice.

She and Alice had come to the hospital at about the same time. Alice was here because she wouldn't eat. She thought she was fat, and if she ate anything, it would make her even more fat. But she *wasn't* fat. Gwen saw Alice in the shower every morning. She was as skinny as a skeleton, the skinniest person Gwen had ever seen. She couldn't understand why Alice wouldn't eat. The food here wasn't as good as Aunt's cooking, but it wasn't that bad, and everyone had to eat, didn't they?

Alice had finally started eating. Gwen felt she had helped with that; she and Alice were best friends. But now Alice was sitting in front of her breakfast tray, her food untouched. Soon she'd be pushing most of it into her paper napkin so she could throw it out later. The staff had stopped watching Alice every minute, so she'd probably get away with it this morning. Losing the gold key had upset Alice, too.

Gwen reached over. "Friends?"

Alice was poking at her food. She didn't look up.

"I'm sorry, Alice. You were right and I was wrong. Okay?"

Alice looked up at Gwen, almost meeting her eyes.

"Friends?" Gwen offered, again.

Just then the new girl, Janet, who was sitting across the table from Gwen and Alice, started crying big, body-jerking tears into her eggs and toast.

"Flood time," Gwen whispered to Alice. "Got your boots?"

It was a private joke between them. Nothing personal against Janet. Tears fell as often on the ward as rain in a rain forest. Gwen had never been to a rain forest in her life, but she imagined it was pretty wet. What was it that Aunt always said?

"If you didn't laugh, you'd have to cry."

A shaky grin built in the corners of Alice's mouth.

"Bring your umbrella?" Alice whispered back.

Gwen started to giggle. And Alice did, too. If you didn't laugh, you'd have to cry—Aunt sure was right about that. Gwen didn't want to think about what was going to happen after breakfast. It just felt good to laugh. Later, she might tell Alice about the cherry-breasted bird, about Mr. Jones finding her, and how she'd discovered the key. Her gold key was gone. She didn't have to keep it a secret anymore.

Gwen looked around the table. All the girls had to sit together at breakfast. At lunch and dinner they could choose. Gwen and Alice always sat together at every meal, even when they were mad at each other.

Janet's tears had dried up. Gwen smiled at her. Mary had eaten everything on her tray, and even put the white paper cap back on top of her empty orange-juice glass. She was rocking forward and back in her place on the bench next to Alice, seeming to stare out at nothing at all. Next to Mary sat Ellen and Beth, friends like Gwen and Alice, whispering about something together. They kept to themselves. Across the table Lynn was talking to her plate. Well, maybe not to her *plate*, but to someone or something that wasn't there. And at the end of the bench sat Ann, shoveling food into her mouth. She looked up at Gwen and frowned, a bit of yellow egg sticking to her lip. Then she started shoveling in food again.

Tap, tap . . .

Gwen looked up. At the head of the table stood Mrs. Libby, one of the attendants on duty this morning.

"Okay, finish up, girls." Was she looking at Alice's lap? Gwen looked, too. Alice had hidden her food in her napkin. Gwen hadn't even seen her do it. At the end of the table Ann jumped up like a soldier at attention, knocking over her half-full glass of orange juice into her last bits of scrambled egg.

"It's okay, hon," Mrs. Libby called down to her. "Sit down and finish. You've got a few more minutes."

Ann slapped down in her seat and started scooping

the wet, eggy orange juice into her mouth with a spoon.

"Gwen, Mrs. West wants you to report to Dr. Stone's office as soon as breakfast is over. Just wait with me until the other girls go. I'll be walking you down."

Gwen liked Mrs. Libby's smile. She was round like Aunt, and soft in her ways, too. It was a relief not to have to face Mrs. West right after breakfast.

But who was Dr. Stone? She'd never heard of him before, or her. You never knew if a doctor was a man or a woman by the name. Her favorite doctor was Dr. Sheela, a small woman from India who wore pale-blue cloth wrapped around and around her. She wore a red spot, like lipstick, on her forehead just above where the eyebrows met, and she spoke with a high, chirpy voice, like a bird's. Gwen loved to hear Dr. Sheela's voice. And she always wore beautiful jewelry. Gwen had wanted to touch the thin gold bracelets that clustered like hoops on Dr. Sheela's wrist. Dr. Sheela would know if Gwen's key was real gold.

Except there wasn't any key to show now. Gwen had to keep reminding herself of that. Keys weren't for patients. Maybe that was why her gold key had disappeared.

"Time, girls," Mrs. Libby said. "You stand with me, Gwen."

Gwen slid out to stand by Mrs. Libby. Alice was next.

Gwen hoped that Mrs. Libby hadn't noticed Alice's napkin, or that Alice hadn't eaten any of the food on her tray. They didn't need to both be in trouble at the same time.

"Hope to see you again in this lifetime," Gwen whispered to Alice.

"Lay a brick," Alice returned.

That's what Gwen loved about Alice. She always had something stupid to say.

The other girls were lining up in the hall, along with the women, to go back to the ward to get their activity assignments for the morning. Gwen walked with Mrs. Libby. She didn't see Mrs. West in her usual place at the head of the line. Today it was another nurse, Miss Moore, who was smoothing down the front of her nurse's uniform with her milk-white hands.

Miss Moore was a real pushover. Everyone said so. If Mrs. West wasn't around to stop it, a girl could get Miss Moore to give in to practically anything. Alice said that Miss Moore had a boyfriend and daydreamed about him all day long; that was why she gave in so quick, so she could go back to thinking about him. Alice was probably right about the boyfriend. Miss Moore was very stylish. And there was something about how she'd give in to a girl for any little thing, as if she couldn't be bothered to say no.

But where was Mrs. West? Gwen's stomach churned as

she walked past the line of girls and women. A few patients watched her go by. Alice caught Gwen's eye and gave her a thumbs-up. Gwen didn't feel like giving a thumbs-up—her heart wouldn't be in it—so she gave back a thumbs-to-the-side.

Gwen followed Mrs. Libby into the stairwell and down the stairs. They stopped at the half-floor landing with the door that opened out to the grounds.

"It's a nice morning to take a walk outside," Mrs. Libby said. She fiddled with her ring of keys, found the one she was looking for, and disarmed the alarm at the door. "No use dragging Mr. Jones out for a second time this morning." She said it kindly, and smiled.

Gwen's tongue loosened, and a flood of questions poured out. "What building are we going to? Who is Dr. Stone? Where is Dr. Sheela? Is she sick?"

"Hold it, hold it." Mrs. Libby was laughing now. "One question at a time."

Gwen hurried to keep up with Mrs. Libby's quick stride as they moved along the concrete sidewalk. The air smelled like grass, and the sun shone through the soft green leaves of the trees. A large black bird cawed as they approached, then flapped away.

"Dr. Stone's office is in Greenlawn," Mrs. Libby said. "He's new."

New? There was always a new doctor at the hospital. Gwen had met with lots of different doctors since coming here. Probably half of them had been new.

"Is he from India?"

"No, I think he's plain ol' American. And a nice man, too, I'm sure. No need to worry, hon."

"Why does he want to talk to me?"

"How about you ask him that when you see him?"

They reached the building called Greenlawn and went inside. Mrs. Libby spoke with the receptionist in the lobby. The receptionist pointed down the corridor.

"Number one oh seven," she said.

They walked down the hallway to a door with the number 107 painted in gold on the frosted glass. Mrs. Libby opened the door. Gwen followed her in.

A woman looked up from a desk, one ear pressed into the end of a telephone receiver. She held up a pink-nail-polished finger, spoke a moment longer, and hung up. She turned her full, smooth face to Gwen.

"And you are?" she asked.

"Gwendolyn Brace," Mrs. Libby said. "Dr. Stone is expecting her."

Gwen could have answered for herself. What did she look like, a baby? Mrs. Libby smiled at Gwen and left. The secretary spoke into the phone again, briefly.

"He'll be out for you in just a moment, Gwendolyn. Why don't you have a seat?" She pointed to two chairs along the wall across from her desk.

"Yes, ma'am." Hardly anyone called her Gwendolyn here, except for Mrs. West. It made this meeting with Dr. Stone feel extra serious.

Just then Dr. Stone's office door opened, and there was Mrs. West in the doorway, saying something into the room in her lecturing tone that buzzed in Gwen's head like a hornet. She noticed Gwen and lowered her voice. Gwen hoped Mrs. West was about to leave, and hoped, too, that whatever the head nurse had said to Dr. Stone, he wouldn't think *too* badly of her at their very first meeting, even though she had broken a number of the ward rules.

But why wasn't she getting a dressing-down in the nurses' office, like the time she'd poured orange juice over Lynn's head for spitting in her oatmeal? Why had she been brought to see Dr. Stone? He didn't even know her. Maybe she'd done something wrong this morning that she didn't even know about.

In the doorway, now, was Dr. Stone. He was tall and broad-shouldered, what Aunt would call "sturdy," with peppered brown-and-gray hair that was sticking out in odd directions. And he wore a bow tie, not tied very straight, either. And no white coat. No jacket at all. If

Gwen hadn't heard Mrs. West saying, "Yes, Doctor . . . Yes, Doctor . . ." all the time, she'd have thought the man couldn't be Dr. Stone. He wore a blue-and-white-striped shirt, unironed by the look of the wrinkles, with a bunch of pens in his shirt breast pocket.

Now he was bowing Mrs. West out of the office door while she was still talking. He looked over his shoulder at Gwen and winked!

"Yes, Mrs. West, absolutely. Yes, yes. Certainly. If I have any questions, I will call the ward right away. Good-bye, Mrs. West. And thank you so much for your concern." He spoke the last part with his head stuck out into the hallway. Then he closed the door, shutting out the sound of Mrs. West's hard-soled shoes clicking down the linoleum. He leaned against the shut door, letting out a long sigh that caused his whole sturdy frame to wilt. Then he sucked in a deep breath and was tall and alive again. His face brightened. He advanced toward Gwen with outstretched hands and a big grin.

"You must be Gwendolyn, am I right?"

"Everyone calls me Gwen."

"Ah, Gwen. Come into my office." He waved his long arm in a sweeping motion, as if to fan Gwen through the door.

CHAPTER SIX

Dr. Stone motioned for Gwen to sit in one of the two chairs facing his desk. It was an almost tidy desk, not heaped with things like some of the other doctors' desks. But Mrs. Libby had said he was new. The rest of his office didn't look like anyone's office yet. The beige walls were bare, with no pictures, calendar, notices, or cards. The metal shelves on the far wall were empty, too, except for a book knocked over on its side, left behind by someone else, probably. And the window had no curtains, not even a pull shade, just a broken metal blind hanging kitty-cornered like a half-opened fan. Dr. Stone should get that fixed.

There wasn't a single plant. Aunt always said that plants cheered up a room. Gwen thought so too. Dr. Stone should get at least one plant. It would grow well on the windowsill, with all that light, as long as he remembered to water it.

Dr. Stone was busy looking over a stack of papers on his desk, her chart probably. He picked up half the stack, carried it over to the chair next to Gwen's, and sat down. She watched him fumble with the loose sheets like a lap full of dried leaves. He had very long arms. Gwen had never met a doctor who didn't sit behind a desk.

It took a while for Dr. Stone to sort all the papers out. Finally, he took in a deep breath, let it out, and looked over in her direction. Their eyes met.

"I wasn't running away," Gwen began, wanting to give her side of the story before Dr. Stone said a word, just in case she didn't get a chance to do it later. Some doctors didn't want patients to talk at all, just to listen. She hoped he wasn't like that. Well, he had listened to Mrs. West. Maybe he would listen to her, too. Should she tell Dr. Stone that a bird had dropped a gold key in the border garden outside her sleeping-room window and she had run out to find it? She didn't even know him. Gwen closed her mouth.

"I believe you, Gwen," Dr. Stone said, sounding as if he really meant it. He grabbed a ballpoint pen from his breast pocket and clicked it.

"I mean, I'm really sorry about going out like that."

"Apology accepted." Dr. Stone shuffled a few more papers on his lap, writing something on the top sheet. Gwen noticed his relaxed hands with their broad-knuckled fingers.

"What will my punishment be?" Mrs. West must

have been speaking with Dr. Stone about it. Why else would she have come to his office before Gwen arrived? Gwen had broken almost all the ward rules she knew about, and probably some she hadn't even heard of before. Why didn't he just get it over with?

"Punishment? No punishment, Gwen. You have apologized for your actions, and I have accepted that apology. Your records show no history of this sort of behavior being usual for you."

"But I don't understand." Had Dr. Stone said she wasn't going to be punished? What would Mrs. West say?

"Listen to me, Gwen." Dr. Stone leaned forward, his elbows resting on the pile of papers in his lap. "Your chart shows that you have never left the ward unattended for any reason before this morning. That you *did* go off the ward without permission just tells me that you had a reason. I'm guessing it was a good one. That's the most logical answer, don't you think?"

Gwen nodded slowly.

"And there was no real harm done, except for a few ruffled feathers." Dr. Stone looked calmly at her from under his bushy eyebrows. "I feel certain that it won't happen again. Am I right, Gwen?"

She nodded her head vigorously now; she wouldn't do *that* again. Dr. Stone's mouth spread into a broad grin.

"Very good then!"

"But what about Mrs. West?"

"Oh, I've settled things with the head nurse. We don't have to say another word about it. Unless"—Dr. Stone met Gwen's eyes—"unless, of course, *you* want to talk about it?" He made it sound as if she really had a choice.

Gwen shook her head. Better to drop the subject altogether.

She watched him take her answer and file it away in his head. His face seemed to whirl and turn like the face of the cuckoo clock in Aunt's kitchen—in goes the little figure on one side of the clock, and out comes a new figure on the other side. Gwen wondered when the clock would strike the hour and the little cuckoo would come out and chirp.

"So!" Dr. Stone looked down at the stack of papers in his lap.

It was time for the little cuckoo to chirp.

"Let's begin by going over a few things from your chart."

Gwen always wished that her chart would become lost so she would never have to "go over a few things" with another doctor again. But that was a wish that never came true. She would have to do it one more time.

"Your full name is Gwendolyn Mary Brace. You were born on March the twentieth—"

"The first day of spring."

"Ah, yes," Dr. Stone said, smiling at Gwen, "in the year 1951. Your parents were Edward and Dorothy Brace, deceased when you were five, almost six, years old."

"And then I went to live with Aunt," Gwen added, quickly.

"Your great-aunt, Mrs. Flora Jewel?"

Gwen nodded. She hardly remembered the time when she hadn't lived with Aunt.

"No brothers or sisters. And you are, now, let me see, you just turned twelve years old in March."

"Aunt came to see me on my birthday."

"Do you know today's date?"

"Yes, it's June eleventh, 1963." Gwen always checked the date on the ward bulletin board outside the day room each morning before going to breakfast. Some girls didn't even know what year it was, let alone the day. Gwen always knew the exact day, even though every day was pretty much the same as every other day on the ward. Today was Tuesday.

"Now, on your admission papers . . ."

Why did she have to go over this again?

". . . under PARENTS' CAUSE OF DEATH, you've written here, 'Atom bomb explosion.'" Dr. Stone looked up at Gwen.

"Aunt wrote it." Gwen felt a fluttering in her stomach. Did they have to talk about this?

"Your aunt wrote it? Was it her idea to write it?"

No. Not her idea at all. Gwen remembered insisting that Aunt write it, yelling at her to get it exactly right. She saw Aunt's eyes again, full of tears.

"I made Aunt write it. Then she started to cry. . . ." Gwen's voice trailed off. She was ashamed about making Aunt cry. Dr. Stone was leaning toward her, as if he were listening with his whole body. He seemed to really want to know, to really care that she explained it right.

"You made your aunt write it, and she started to cry."

Yes, that's how it was. She nodded.

"Why do you think it made her cry?"

"What?"

Everyone else had asked Gwen why she made Aunt write it, not why it had made Aunt cry. She wondered now, why *had* Aunt cried just then?

"Because she was worried about the radioactivity? You know, from the fallout. I was there. But if I was radioactive, wouldn't I glow in the dark? I don't, you know. I've checked. That's what I kept telling Aunt, so she wouldn't worry. But she still did."

"It says, in parentheses, 'Aunt reports patient's parents died in an automobile accident on January twelfth, 1957.'"

The faces of her mother and father laughing in the front seat of the big station wagon, smiling toward each other in her mind, caused Gwen's stomach to lurch and grip at her insides. She shook the picture away. Then she heard in her memory the air-raid horn with its long, thin wail filling the halls of her school. It was last fall, just before the Halloween party. Mrs. Perry had made them crawl under their desks. Gwen hadn't felt comfortable at all under her desk in her black witch's costume. She'd had to take off her witch's hat with the scraggly orange hair so she could fit into the small, cramped space. She hadn't wanted to take it off. Her witch's hat had made her feel like a witch, scary and full of powerful magic to fend off an attack. Without it she was just Gwen. It was at that moment, crouched under her school desk waiting for the Bomb to drop on her head, that she suddenly knew the real reason for her parents' death.

"Gwen?"

Gwen broke out of her thoughts to see Dr. Stone looking at her.

"That's why they call me 'the atom bomb girl.'"

"Who calls you that?"

"The women on the ward, and some of the girls. Well, they *did* call me that. They don't anymore."

Gwen remembered every bit of the explosion: driving in the car, the wintry landscape flying by, her mother turning to her father, her father's hand reaching out; then the flash of light, the eerie quiet, the feeling of flying through the air and landing hard. The sound rushed back, the noise, the soot like black grease all over her clothes and body, the pain in her elbow, a siren's whine—Gwen clapped her hands over her ears—and the ash, the gray ash coming out of the sky, and the horrible smell of burning. She remembered the cold, the fire and the cold, the soot on white snow.

Her heart was pounding, and she was breathing fast. Gwen watched Dr. Stone move his chair closer to hers and felt her heart hitting in her chest like it was banging to get out. She pushed the vision away.

It took Aunt days to scrub off all the soot.

"They threw my clothes away. But Aunt sewed me new ones. She sews all my clothes, except now I'm learning to sew my own. I only have a little scar." Gwen held out her right elbow, trying to hold it steady for Dr. Stone to see. Along the elbow bone was a thin bluish-white line.

"Alice, my best friend, says that no one can survive an atom bomb attack, but . . ." Gwen's eyes darted to look at Dr. Stone. "But I don't think about any of that now. That's why I get to go home soon, right?"

"Gwen, have any of the staff said that you might be going home soon?"

"Well, no." But she was fine. Everyone could see that. Why not let her go home? She wouldn't make Aunt cry again.

Gwen held her hands in her lap, rubbing her fingers together, aware that they were tingling from clutching her hands too tightly into fists. She tried to slow her breathing, to show Dr. Stone that everything was fine. And the tingling was going away; she was calming down. But something other than just her fingers was moving in her hand. Gwen looked down. There, its little snake of chain sliding over and around, was her gold key.

Her eyes flew up to see Dr. Stone watching her closely. Had he seen the key? She covered it with her other hand, hoping to hide it.

"Gwen—"

She jumped, startled by his voice.

"Can we finish now?" She needed to get her key secretly away. She could talk to Dr. Stone another time.

"Gwen, listen to me. I don't think it's the right time to be sending you home. Soon, Gwen, we all hope for that. But not right now. Do you understand?"

Not right now, but soon . . .

Had Dr. Stone just said she would be going home soon? Gwen's face broke into a smile. She nodded her head. Yes, she understood that.

"But can we finish now?" she asked, again.

"Yes, that would be fine. Do you have any questions, Gwen?"

"No." No questions at all.

Gwen's legs felt rubbery as she stood up. She followed Dr. Stone out to the secretary's office. While his back was turned as he spoke to Miss Avery, Gwen slipped the key and chain over her head and tucked it under her blouse, pulling her collar up snugly so the chain wouldn't show. She liked Dr. Stone. And not just because he said she might be going home soon. Dr. Stone reminded Gwen of a tall tree standing firm in the wind.

And her gold key was back! Gwen was so happy, she reached out and hugged Dr. Stone. He felt as solid as a tree. But she pulled back almost instantly. Hugging, any touching, was against the rules, just like going barefoot.

"Sorry."

"No harm done, Gwen," he said. "Miss Avery will call the ward for an escort. And if you have any questions later on, just ask someone at the nurses' station to reach me. All right?"

Gwen nodded. She watched the door to Dr. Stone's office shut tight.

CHAPTER SEVEN

Gwen sat down in a chair across from Miss Avery's desk, the same one she'd sat in earlier that morning when Mrs. Libby had brought her here. Miss Avery was talking on the phone. She hung up.

"Someone will be coming to pick you up in a little bit," Miss Avery said. "Would you like a peppermint?" The secretary reached into a side drawer and pulled out a red-and-white-striped candy wrapped in cellophane. She handed it over the desk to Gwen.

"Thank you."

Aunt had always taught Gwen to say "thank you" when someone gave her something, even if she didn't want it. She disliked peppermints. But it was nice of Miss Avery anyway. Maybe Alice would like it? She'd save it and give it to Alice when she saw her before lunch.

As Gwen waited, she looked out the window. Dr. Stone's office was on the first floor facing the wide front lawn of the hospital grounds. White clouds floated across the blue sky, the puffy kind that Aunt called fair-weather clouds.

Fair weather. That seemed just about right.

Gwen imagined herself writing a letter to Aunt cut out of the fair-weather clouds so that the blue showed through. And Aunt would look up while she hung out the wash on the line, maybe to stretch her back or just to watch the clouds move by, and there she'd see what Gwen had written to her: *Coming home soon. Love, Gwen.* It would be like Gwen was moving along with the clouds, too.

She wished she could lie outside in the grass right now. Watching the sky though a window just wasn't the same as being outdoors, where the clouds felt bigger and closer. Watching the sky from indoors was a lot like looking at a photograph album: pretty, but not the same thing. Dr. Stone had said she would be going home soon. Then she could stay outdoors all day if she liked, the whole summer long. Gwen started swinging her feet under the chair. The tips of her sneakers stuttered across the linoleum floor.

Gwen wished she could go home right away. And why not? What was going to change in her from this week to the next? If she was well enough to go home soon, why not send her home *now*?

She should have asked Dr. Stone about going home

right away, asked him while they were in his office. Should she ask Miss Avery to get him now? He had said to be sure to reach him with any questions she might have. And it would hardly be going out of his way to step into his secretary's office, just for a moment, so she could speak with him. It would be a lot easier than his coming up to the ward.

Gwen looked over at Miss Avery. She was putting a piece of paper in the typewriter.

"Miss Avery?"

Miss Avery looked up at Gwen and smiled.

"I was wondering if—"

Suddenly the door to the hallway opened, and there was Mrs. West.

"Come along now, Gwendolyn." She didn't bother to step into the office.

Mrs. West never came to escort anyone to and from the ward. She was the head nurse. That meant she just bossed everyone around. That's what Alice said, anyway. What was she doing here?

"Gwendolyn, come along."

"Yes, ma'am."

Gwen got up and walked toward Mrs. West, who was waiting in the doorway. The head nurse was carrying a manila envelope in one hand.

"Good-bye, Gwen," Miss Avery said.

"'Bye," Gwen said, raising the fingers of one hand in Miss Avery's direction. She couldn't manage a smile. Her eyes lingered for a moment on the closed door to Dr. Stone's office.

"Gwendolyn?" Mrs. West was waiting.

Gwen pulled her eyes away from the office door and followed the head nurse down the hall.

They walked outside, the same way she and Mrs. Libby had walked earlier that morning. At a crossroads in the sidewalk, the head nurse turned, walking away from Pineview and the ward. Gwen scurried to catch up.

"Aren't we going back to the ward?"

"I have something to drop off at the Main Building. We'll go there first."

Gwen usually loved walking outside whenever she could get the chance. The longer the walk, the better. But walking with Mrs. West wasn't any fun at all. Gwen wanted to go back to the ward. She was disappointed, too, that she hadn't been able to talk to Dr. Stone about going home. If she were home right now, she could sit in the kitchen and sew, or go outside if she felt like it, all by herself. Here, she couldn't go anywhere by herself except to the toilet, and only there after she'd asked. At least she was allowed that. Lots of girls and women on the ward had to have an escort just to go to the toilet. Even Alice.

Why Alice needed an escort, Gwen could never figure out. She'd asked her about it soon after they became friends. Alice had just shrugged her shoulders.

"I dunno" was all she said.

Large hemlocks surrounded the Main Building. The bright green of the new needles sparkled against the old red brick like glitter on a birthday card. If it hadn't been for the presence of Mrs. West, Gwen imagined, she would be feeling perfectly content right now with the sky, the trees, and the warmth of the sun on her face and arms.

The Main Building was larger than the other buildings at the hospital; it seemed older, too, than Pineview. Looking through the hemlocks, Gwen could see a flock of pigeons nesting high up in the heavy white trim, under the eaves of the sharp-angled roof. It was a beautiful old building, but a little frightening, too. It was the place people came when they were being committed to the hospital, the place where Aunt had brought her when Gwen had come to stay.

The word "committed" didn't sound as nice to Gwen as "admitted." Alice had said that "admitted" meant you had a choice and "committed" meant that you were forced, and anyone who came to a place like this by choice was crazy enough to be forced to stay. Then she laughed and laughed. Gwen didn't understand what was so funny. Didn't everyone have a choice about coming to the hospital, every grown-up, that is? Wasn't it written in the Constitution of the United States of America? She had learned about the Constitution from her teacher at school, Mrs. Perry. Alice had laughed even harder when Gwen said that. Then Gwen had laughed, too. It was hard for Gwen not to laugh along with Alice, even when she didn't understand what was so funny.

Gwen had been inside the Main Building only two other times, first when Aunt had brought her here in the winter, and then, on her birthday, when Aunt had come for a visit. The Main Building was the place where all the girls and women came to meet visitors from home; families never came on the ward. Alice said they were kept off the ward because if they saw the squalor that their dear daughter or son or husband or wife was living in here, they would scoop them right up and out of the hospital that very instant—making a scene of it, too. Then there wouldn't be any patients in the hospital, and all the staff would be out of a job.

Alice said the craziest things.

Gwen wondered if the Main Building was the place a patient went when she was going *home* from the hospital, too. Was Mrs. West taking Gwen to the Main Building to help arrange for her going home? Suddenly the presence of Mrs. West to collect Gwen at Dr. Stone's office began to make sense.

She glanced at the envelope the head nurse was carrying. Were her going-home papers in it? Why else would Mrs. West have come to escort her back to the ward? Gwen couldn't think of a single other reason. She tried to get a look at the front of the envelope to see if her name was written on it, but Mrs. West was holding it tightly to her side, opposite the side where Gwen walked. She didn't dare change sides to get a better look. That wouldn't be a good idea, especially if there was a chance that the papers in the envelope were for her going home.

Gwen hurried to walk right beside Mrs. West. No lagging behind today! She hadn't needed to speak to Dr. Stone after all.

CHAPTER EIGHT

Mrs. West opened one of the large oak doors into the Main Building and walked in. Gwen followed behind her. The only other time she'd walked through these doors was when she and Aunt had come to the hospital to bring Gwen to stay. Gwen remembered the feeling, as if she had entered a cave. She felt the same way now. Dark wood closed in around her, shutting out the bright-blue day.

The entry hall was cavernous and smelled of wood polish. Stuffed leather chairs were arranged in groups of four or five, and oil portraits of men in dark suits hung steady in their gilt frames along the paneled walls. A heavily carved reception desk filled the far right corner, where a woman stood, dressed in a white uniform and starched cap, looking through half glasses into an open book. Gwen imagined the lobby of a grand hotel might look like this: elegant, old, and very, very hushed.

She followed Mrs. West past the reception desk and down the large central corridor into the interior of the Main Building. The head nurse was checking labels on the doors as they walked. She stopped at the door marked RECORDS OFFICE and opened it. They went in.

The Records Office was much brighter than the corridor. Double lines of bare fluorescent bulbs flickered on the ceiling, illuminating rows and rows of metal shelves packed with paper-filled folders. The shelves reached to the very tip-top of the high plaster ceiling. Gwen had never seen so many sheets of paper in one place in her life! There was a narrow counter in front of the shelves, and behind the counter stood a man in a brown suit. He looked up and smiled at Mrs. West. Gwen noticed a ladder leaning against the side wall.

Mrs. West pointed to a chair by the door and told Gwen to sit. Then the head nurse walked up to the counter and handed the envelope she was carrying to the man. They spoke quietly. Gwen couldn't hear what they were saying. It had never occurred to her before this morning that Mrs. West did anything but order around the patients and staff on the ward. She even seemed on friendly terms with the man in the brown suit. He took the folder and walked over to the ladder. Resting it on his shoulder, he carried the ladder down the center row of shelves, looking for something over his head.

"Mackenzie, did you say?" he called back to Mrs. West.

Mackenzie? That wasn't Gwen's name. Gwen's hopes

for going home tipped over and spilled across the Records Office floor.

"Ah, yes, here it is," the man said. He leaned the ladder against the shelf and climbed a few steps up to reach for something. "Alice Mackenzie. Here it is. I'll take care of it right away." He pulled the folder from the shelf and waved it at Mrs. West with a smile.

Alice?

What was he going to take care of right away? Were they going to send Alice home? Gwen hoped for Alice's going home—of course she hoped for that—but it didn't make any sense. Alice was always saying she was going to go home, in a day, or a week, but Gwen knew she was making it up, just another one of Alice's stories. Alice hadn't even eaten her breakfast this morning.

"Thank you," Mrs. West said to the man on the ladder. Then, "Gwendolyn, come along."

"Mrs. West, why was he talking about Alice? Is she going home?" Gwen jumped out of her chair and followed the head nurse out of the Records Office.

"Mrs. West?"

They didn't turn back the way they had come but headed in the opposite direction, down the corridor, away from the front doors of the Main Building. This was the way Gwen had been taken to the ward when she had first come here, and both coming and going from her visit to Aunt. This was the way to the north tunnel that led back to Pineview, underground.

"Is Alice all right?"

Gwen remembered Alice at breakfast this morning, with her napkin full of food. No one else had noticed any of that, just herself. Or had they? She wouldn't tell when Alice didn't eat. Not unless she stopped eating all the time. That wouldn't be healthy for Alice; even Gwen knew that. Then she would have to tell someone. But not Mrs. West. Mrs. West never listened anyway.

They came to the entrance into the north tunnel. Mrs. West opened the door and held it for Gwen to pass through; a yellow-and-black FALLOUT SHELTER sign was riveted to the wall by the doorway. As they walked down the slope and into the brick-walled tunnel, Gwen slipped a hand under the collar of her blouse, to check for her gold key. Her fingers bumped along the string of tiny pop beads, smooth and warm from being so close to her skin. She let out a long breath; her shoulders relaxed. She had probably overreacted just now. Of course, Alice was fine. They must move Alice's chart all over the place, just like they did her own. Gwen's chart had been moved to Dr. Stone's office this morning. It would probably be sent back to the Records Office this afternoon, or brought to the ward.

As for her going home, Gwen would ask to speak to

Dr. Stone when she got back to the ward, maybe before lunch. She was sure she could make him see the sense of letting her go home right away.

Gwen glanced up at the brick arches overhead. She always felt safer underground. Once she'd gone home with a girl from school, not a friend, just someone to stay with one afternoon when Aunt had to be away. After a snack, the girl had told Gwen, "Come on!" and led her down to the basement and through a cinder-block entry-way. A light switch clicked, and Gwen found herself standing in a little concrete room. It looked like a doll's house with bunk beds, a table and chairs, a sofa, and a kitchenette, but life-sized. Along one of the concrete walls were metal shelves full of canned goods, cereal boxes, a bucket and tools: odd things. There were even jigsaw puzzles and a checkerboard. On another wall was a radio, with headphones, sitting on a little shelf, and hanging next to the radio was a photograph of the American flag flying against a blue, blue sky. There were no windows.

"It's a *bomb shelter*," the girl had told Gwen, "in case of an attack." The room had a thick concrete ceiling and cinder-block walls, strong enough, she told Gwen, to withstand a direct hit. And who knew when the Bomb was coming? Her father said that these days it paid to be prepared.

As they had turned to leave, Gwen had looked up.

Mounted on the wall above the doorway was a shotgun on a metal rack—

"Gwendolyn, stop dawdling and come along."

"What? Oh. Sorry, Mrs. West." Gwen scurried to catch up with the head nurse, who was already a few archways ahead.

Maybe she should count linoleum tiles as she walked along, to keep herself more alert. It was a game Gwen played sometimes, stepping in the center of a tile, never on a crack. Alice wouldn't play it with her on the ward; she called it "infantile." Gwen measured her steps to fit every three tiles, that was easy, then every four, then five, no, that was too far to reach. Gwen started stepping on every single tile, on her tiptoes. Baby steps.

"Stop whatever it is you are doing, Gwendolyn, and walk normally."

"Yes, ma'am." Gwen stopped counting tiles.

She and Aunt didn't have a bomb shelter at home, just a root cellar dug underneath the summer kitchen at the back of the house. The root cellar was where they stored the potatoes and other root vegetables that Aunt grew in the vegetable plot, to keep them cool and fresh through the winter months. The root cellar didn't have a concrete ceiling, or even a dirt one, just the rough underside of the plank wood floor of the summer kitchen. So much light came into the cellar through the cracks in the floorboards that Gwen never had to take a flashlight when she went down to get potatoes or a cabbage or some carrots for the dinner. There was nothing strong at all about the root-cellar ceiling. It would never survive a direct hit, or any other kind of hit, either.

Maybe she and Alice could play cards before lunch, after she'd talked with Dr. Stone. They always played crazy eights, Gwen's favorite. Alice didn't mind what game they played and always let Gwen choose. For her part, Gwen tried not to mind when Alice cheated sometimes. It was an even trade.

They had played crazy eights later that afternoon at her schoolmate's house, too. Gwen had just finished her turn when she found the words to ask the question that had been on her mind ever since they had come up from the girl's basement. Could Gwen, Gwen *and* Aunt, come and stay in the bomb shelter with the girl and her family, if there was an atom bomb attack? They didn't have a bomb shelter of their own.

It was the girl's turn, and she laid an eight on top of the pile.

"Hearts," she said, grinning.

Gwen didn't have any hearts and the girl knew it, or an eight, so she started picking up cards from the pile.

Could they? Gwen had asked again, urgently.

"No," the girl said, watching Gwen pick up card after

card from the pile, "and if you try to come in, my father will have to shoot you. That's what the shotgun is for."

The door into Pineview was straight ahead. Mrs. West opened it. She held the door for Gwen to pass through, then walked briskly up the stairs. Gwen followed the head nurse. Maybe Alice was in the sleeping room waiting for her to get back? She'd check in with Alice about playing cards, then ask to speak to Dr. Stone at the nurses' station.

They reached the third-floor stairwell and walked onto the ward. Gwen hurried across the hallway. Her sneakers squeaked on the shiny linoleum floor as she skidded around the door frame and into the girls' sleeping room.

"Alice, do you want to—" Gwen stopped cold.

In Alice's sleeping area was a rolled-up mattress on bare bedsprings. The nightstand was cleared. The clothespegs on the wall were empty.

CHAPTER NINE

Gwen ran from the sleeping room into the hall.

"Stop running, please," a day nurse called out.

Gwen slowed her feet, but her heart raced ahead. Where was Alice? She walked quickly past the nurses' station—the staff wouldn't tell her anything; she knew the rules—and into the day room, where the girls would be assembling for lunch. Gwen saw Mary sitting in a chair by the far wall. She rushed over to her.

"Where's Alice? All of her things are gone." Mary was rocking back and forth in the padded day room chair as if she hadn't heard Gwen. Gwen reached out and shook Mary; she stopped rocking. "Look at me! Where is Alice?"

"Lower voices, please," another day nurse called out.

Gwen lowered her voice and with both hands raised Mary's face to look at her own. "What's happened to her, Mary? *Please!*"

"Dead," Mary whispered, her eyes angled downward at the floor. Gwen let go of Mary's head.

Alice was *dead*? No. She wouldn't believe that.

"Why did you say that, Mary? Think what you're saying!"

Janet, who was standing next to Mary, started to cry.

"What *happened*, Janet?"

"She, she fell over, like she was, like she was, dead, or sick, or . . ." The words heaved out of Janet. "She, um, someone came and put her on a stretcher, like an ambulance one, they, um, and they, um, they took her away. Her eyes were closed. I saw her eyes were closed. She was, she was sh-sh-shaking, too."

"If she was shaking, then she couldn't be dead." Gwen hurried out of the day room. Miss Moore was sitting alone at the nurses' station. She raced up to the desk; she would *make* Miss Moore tell.

"I want to know what's happened to Alice." Gwen pressed her palms down hard on the wooden desktop. "Tell me where she is."

Miss Moore shifted uneasily in her chair. "I'm sorry, Gwen. That's confidential information. You know I can't . . ."

Gwen gripped Miss Moore with her eyes. A small crowd of patients gathered around them.

"Um, well, you see, Gwen . . ."

"I will take care of this, Nurse Moore." It was Mrs. West.

"Where did you take Alice?" Gwen glared at Mrs. West. "Tell me what's happened to her. Tell me!"

"Gwendolyn, it goes against hospital policy for members of the staff to discuss the condition of any patient with any other patient. I am certain you are aware of that."

"But Alice—" They were *best friends*; Gwen had a right to know!

"The rules on confidentiality protect all patients, Gwendolyn, including yourself. Now, I suggest you go back into the day room and find something to do until the lunch call."

"I will not!" Gwen stamped her foot down hard; the rubber sole of her sneaker squeaked as it hit the linoleum floor. "I want to speak to Dr. Stone. He told me to ask for him if I needed anything or had any questions. I want to speak to him now."

"That is out of the question, Gwendolyn. He told you no such thing."

"I want to speak with Dr. Stone!" How dare Mrs. West say that—he *did* tell her!

"You will speak with the doctor at your scheduled appointment, just like everyone else."

"I want to speak to Dr. Stone *now!*"

"Do as you are told, Gwendolyn."

"What have you done with Alice? What have you done with her?" Gwen screamed.

"Gwendolyn! Control your temper immediately!"

"Tell me! Tell me!"

The crowd of patients tightened in a circle around Gwen. Miss Moore stepped forward and put a hand on her shoulder.

"Come on, Gwen," she coaxed.

Gwen shrugged her off and lunged at Mrs. West, grabbing at the head nurse's starched white sleeves, trying to shake the words out.

"Tell me!"

Hands lifted Gwen away. She wrested her arms and kicked out her feet, but she could not get free.

"Let me speak to Dr. Stone!"

Her arms were being forced into a muslin shirt. Gwen pulled one arm out. Someone grabbed it again. A strong hand held her wrist tight.

"Ow!"

Gwen leaned over and bit the shoulder of the hand squeezing her wrist and forcing her arm into the long sleeve.

"Why you little . . ."

It was a woman's voice close behind her ear. Gwen tried to pull her other arm out of the shirt as thick muslin cloth whipped around her, crisscrossing her arms like a pretzel across her chest. She tugged and grunted, but could not move her arms. A hard knot cinched into the center of her back as the empty lengths of sleeve were tied tight.

Someone picked Gwen up from behind and began walking her away from the nurses' station. Gwen whipped her head from side to side, kicking her legs out hard.

"Let go of me!"

A male attendant Gwen hadn't seen before caught her legs and held them tight to his chest. They carried her down the hallway. A patient laughed. Gwen heard the jingle of keys and a door swish open; she was carried into a room and set down flat on the hard floor. Hands pinned her there for a moment at her shoulders and ankles. Gwen closed her eyes. Then the hands let go. She listened to the quick shuffle of feet and a door shutting tight. Keys clinked, metal drums slipped and fell into place. Then silence.

Gwen opened her eyes. She was alone in a room.

Anger rushed through her like a chimney fire. "Let me out! I want to speak with Dr. Stone! What have you done to Alice? Let me out! Let me out! Let me out!"

Gwen's screams wore down to a hoarse whisper, then no voice at all, just a heap of knotted muslin on the bare linoleum floor.

After a while Gwen managed to sit up. The room was small, and the walls were bare. A single lightbulb in the center of the ceiling shone yellow through a wire casing that cast shadows on the walls and floor of the room like bars moving out from the ceiling, down the walls, and across the floor. The bars of shadow surrounded Gwen like a cage.

The acrid smell of old urine, much stronger than in the toilet room, seared her nostrils. There was no furniture, only a bare mattress on the floor in the far corner. No window looked into the room, just a small, wire-embedded rectangle of glass set high up in the locked metal door. Gwen supposed that was for the attendant to check on the crazy lunatic inside.

So this was the "quiet room." A rush of humiliation flooded through Gwen. She had heard about the quiet room; Alice called it "the jail"; poor Alice! But Gwen had never imagined herself being locked inside. No one would tell her what had happened to Alice, now. As for speaking with Dr. Stone—they were not going to let her go home after this.

A face peered into the quiet room through the small glass rectangle in the door. It was one of the attendants who had put her in, the man who held her feet. She stared back at him with eyes that must look like she felt; not Gwen, not even human, just a thing to be stared at. Gwen turned away. She didn't want to watch herself being stared at anymore. She wondered how long they would keep her here. Through lunch? For the rest of her life?

Gwen realized, suddenly, that she couldn't hear anything going on outside her small cell. If it didn't stink so badly, she thought she might prefer the quiet of this room to the noise on the ward. The silence felt like a bundle of quilts wrapped around and around her, padding her against everything that hurt. Alice was gone. Dr. Stone was as good as gone, her going home surely taken away. She had no power to change any of it; she just had the quiet.

And her gold key?

Had they taken away her key? Gwen's hands were bound, so she couldn't feel for it. She checked to see if the attendant was still looking in at her. He wasn't. She shook her body. Maybe she could feel the key shift under her blouse.

Please let it still be there.

But nothing shifted, no motion at all. Gwen tried pushing her arms out against the tight muslin shirt to make a space for the key to move in. She rocked from side to side. Yes, she could feel it! The chain rolled along the back of her neck. And hanging from it, she felt the weight of gold.

The staff on the ward didn't know about her key yet, but they would. That's just how it was around here. Then they'd take away her gold key, too.

It must be lunchtime now, but Gwen didn't feel hungry, just very tired. Maybe she should lie down? She inched herself over to the mattress, but changed her mind when she got a whiff of it. It reeked of disinfectant and urine. Gwen moved to the other side of the small room, as far away from the mattress as possible. With her arms tied to her chest and the knot cinched hard against her back, she could only lie on her side. So she did, turning her face away from the little glass window in the door. Her thoughts drifted to Alice at breakfast this morning. "Lay a brick," Alice had said, touching Gwen's hand with her own; Alice's fingers had felt as thin and dry as twigs.

Gwen was getting uncomfortable lying on the floor. She sat up and leaned against the wall; that was better. What in the world would Aunt think of her now, tied up like a mean dog in a smelly old shed, locked up like one of Alice's lunatics and murderers? She'd really disgraced herself this time, disgraced Aunt, too. All the trust and love Aunt had wrapped around her year after loving year, all ending with this. As tired as Gwen felt, she couldn't sleep. There was so much to think about.

Well, that's what she would do then. Think.

She couldn't do one other thing.

Gwen thought about Alice. If Alice had been taken away on an ambulance stretcher, did that mean she was at a different hospital? This was a big hospital. Maybe there was a ward for sick people here, sick in their bodies, not just in their minds. Gwen imagined nurses bustling around Alice, not starchy nurses like Mrs. West, but nice, soft nurses who would attend to Alice's every need. She hoped Alice was in a sick ward here.

Gwen thought about Aunt. What would Aunt be doing right now? Gwen imagined her sitting at the kitchen table, one hand resting on a sheet of white paper, holding it steady; the other gripping the fat, black fountain pen, holding a thought: *Dearest Gwennie . . .*

Aunt had taught Gwen how to fill the reservoir in the fountain pen, first lifting, then pressing the metal lever on the pen shaft as the nib drew in the ink. In the opened bottle the glassy ink looked iridescent, like a blue-black pool to make a wish on. Gwen wished she could be with Aunt right now, telling her stories about Alice and the other girls on the ward, about mean Mrs. West; then Aunt would fold Gwen in her arms and hug and hug her. All Gwen could feel now were her own arms wrapped across her chest and tied.

It seemed strange. When you were really bad here, they tied your arms in a way that made you hug yourself. Gwen wanted a hug from Aunt so much that it hurt. But she couldn't have that, not for a long time. Maybe never again. She'd just have to make do with a hug from herself. She'd have to pretend it was Aunt.

Pretending was another thing not allowed on the ward. No pretending that Aunt's arms were around her, or that she might be going home soon. No pretending anything that wasn't real. But who was going to stop her here? And what could they do to her, anyway? Everything was gone now. Well, everything but her gold key, and the staff would take that away as soon as they discovered it. Then she'd be free of them, free of the ward. Free. What an odd thing, after being bound and tied and locked in this stinking room—after all that.

Gwen's thoughts settled on the soft features of Aunt's face. She rested her head against the smooth plaster wall, trying to get comfortable. But something on the wall was poking into her cheek. Gwen shifted a little bit away, leaning her head against another spot on the wall, but that, too, felt poky and rough. She straightened up to have a look and was immediately confused. The wall by her face that should have been a smooth, white plaster was now grayish brown and corklike; deep gouges moved vertically, like knife hacks, up and down the jagged surface.

Turning back to look around the dimly lit room, she saw the door with its single window, the overhead lamp, the cage of light just as it had been before. Gwen didn't think she'd ever be glad to see the quiet room. But for a moment she was.

And then, suddenly, *it wasn't.*

Gwen watched with alarm as the familiar space began to wisp away like shrouds of fog. The quiet room, now a shredding of wall and ceiling and door, seemed to hang like rips of netting draped over rods. But there weren't any rods. And behind the cage-lit space of the room was something unbelievable. The room gaped, not into nothingness, not into the ward, the attendant sitting outside the door, the hall, the sleeping rooms beyond, not into the hospital or outside it, either; the room was dissolving, literally, impossibly, into a day-lit clearing of trees.

She was in a forest.

Gwen turned her head, looking at where her cheek had leaned against the plaster wall. The wall was gone, and in its place was the rough, gouged bark of a very large tree.

This didn't seem possible.

Gwen looked up at what should have been the ceiling, roof, and beyond that, the blue sky above Pineview. Instead, she saw the dark, broad limbs and soft, green leaves of a living tree, right in the quiet room.

But not the quiet room anymore.

Gwen pinched herself on the arm and felt it. Then she realized what she had just done and looked down to see both her hands unbound and resting on her lap. A cool breeze skimmed over her face and arms; it felt delicious. She wasn't in the muslin shirt anymore, or even, it seemed, anywhere familiar at all. She was Gwen, sitting against a large tree in a forest. The strangest part was knowing for certain that she wasn't in the quiet room, on the ward, or anywhere in the hospital at all.

She was just here.

CHAPTER TEN

Gwen stood up. Her legs felt stiff. Bits of stems and leaves clung to her dungarees where she'd been kneeling on the ground. She turned slowly, looking all around her. The mist, or whatever it was, had completely cleared now, and the silence of the forest, when Gwen stood very still, was more quiet than ten quiet rooms boxed together.

She took a few steps. Small twigs snapped under her sneakers—the sound seemed real enough. Gwen turned and looked at the tree. It was an oak, she was sure of it, and old because the trunk was so wide. Acorns dotted the ground; some were broken caps from nuts, some whole. She leaned down and picked up a cluster of acorns on a twig; the honey-brown nuts, topped with their umber caps, reminded Gwen of home. She slipped the twig into her pocket.

Should she be afraid? Because she wasn't.

Gwen held out her empty hands to look at them, to check that they were hers, released from the muslin shirt. All around her the forest was coming to life. Gwen could feel it, like a first, deep breath, then in and out: the earth breathing.

She was wearing the same clothes she'd had on before they put her in the quiet room, her blue blouse, denim dungarees, white anklets, and sneakers. Gwen reached under the collar of her blouse for the gold key hanging on its chain.

She still had her key.

Under the big oak the ground was clear. Dried leaves and moss spread out like a circle cloth under its heavy branches. An occasional threadbare root stitched through the papery brown leaves and mats of green. All the other trees growing around the oak were tall and thin—Aunt would have called them spindly—with lots of thick brush underneath. And close to her was an odd-looking thing.

A tree?

Gwen reached out to touch it. The surface felt too cold for bark, too sharp, more like metal than wood. She looked up. No, not a tree!

It was a lamppost.

But a lamppost, here?

The overall color of the post was rust brown, but where flakes of shiny enamel still held, Gwen could see that it had once been painted a deep forest green. Four large panes of glass made up the lamp; one was cracked right through. Dried leaves had collected inside it, making a nest for the single lightbulb, sheared from its socket, a decapitated, whitish egg-blue.

She wished she could bring Aunt here, it was so quiet and lovely. The moist air felt like a gentle hand touching her face. But she didn't even know her way here, let alone her way back to Aunt to bring her here too. She had no idea at all.

Gwen slipped the gold key and chain up over her head and let it sift between her open fingers, from one hand to the other. The string of small balls chinked against the soft gold. The metal felt warm from being so close to her skin . . . *chink, chink* . . . the sound was lulling and famil-iar . . . *chink, chink* . . . as gold and bead chain poured in and over her hands.

Then the sound moved . . . *chink, chink* . . . wisped away from Gwen's hand like bird flight . . . *chink, chink* . . . coming from somewhere else.

Then silence.

Gwen turned and looked behind her. A one-eyed door came into view, blotting out the air and trees. She tried to slip the gold key back over her head, but her arms were bound. Gwen looked down and saw no key in her hands, no hands. Over her blue blouse was the horrid muslin shirt.

A bare overhead bulb filtered yellow man-made light

into a small room. The light irritated her eyes. And the air—what a stench! The unmistakable smell of urine brought Gwen back to that other place. She knew where she was now.

The lock bolt giving way sounded like a screech.

Gwen's stomach growled noisily. What time was it? She was hungry and stiff all over. She wanted to stretch but could not. Her arms felt absent across her chest.

And the forest was gone.

Gwen heard a handle click and the door swish open. A flood of noise washed in. What an irritating racket! Had the ward always been this loud? Gwen singled out a voice speaking to her.

"Gwendolyn." It was Mrs. West. "You may rejoin the others, but first you must apologize."

What had Mrs. West asked her to do?

"Gwendolyn?"

Gwen remembered Alice and pressed her lips tightly together; she shook her head. She would not apologize for wanting to know what had happened. Poor Alice! How could she apologize for that?

"I see."

Mrs. West called into the hallway. "Nurse Moore, you may remove the straitjacket and escort Gwendolyn to the toilet, and stay with her. After that, take her to the small activities room." She turned back to Gwen. "There you can think a little more about the need to apologize. A dinner tray will be brought up from the dining hall."

Gwen turned her face away from Mrs. West. She didn't stand, or even look around, when Miss Moore came and began untying the knot at the center of her back. Gwen felt the wrappings loosen around her chest as the muslin shirt slipped away. Her arms dropped like weights from her stiff shoulders.

"Flap your arms around, Gwen," Miss Moore said. "It gets the circulation going quicker."

Gwen allowed herself to be helped up. Her arms were her arms, but they didn't feel like a part of her at all. As she flapped them up and down, the circulation began to return. Now she could feel them! Pins and needles raced up and down Gwen's arms, pinpricks from her shoulders all the way to the tips of her fingers.

Miss Moore put a hand on Gwen's shoulder and walked her out of the quiet room and into the overbright hallway. Gwen squinted for a moment as her eyes adjusted to the light.

But what had happened to the day? How long had she been in the quiet room?

As Gwen passed a window on her way to the toilet room, she looked out. The sky wasn't blue anymore; it was greenish-gray, and dark. A storm was coming. Miss

Moore tugged lightly for Gwen to come along, but Gwen's eyes clung to the window even as the rest of her body was being pulled away. A streak of lightning cracked through the air. She watched the thread of yellow electricity come to ground—

BOOM!

A gasp rose from the girls and women on the ward, creating its own electric charge. The shuffling of shoes and ward slippers filled the hall like rustling leaves. It was a close hit. Now the rain *whooshed* down in a free-for-all, pelting against the wire-embedded glass, washing away the view.

Miss Moore led Gwen to the toilet room as the wind began blowing into the ward, first soft and low, then building to a terrible shriek, finding its way in through every crevice and corner of each old wooden window sash. Another crack of lightning—*BOOM!* Some of the patients on the ward were shrieking too.

Free-for-all—*BOOM!*

Miss Moore opened the door to the toilet room for Gwen. As it closed, the sound of the wind was muffled somewhat; there were no windows in the toilet room. Gwen raced into a stall. She knew Mrs. West's orders meant that she was to be watched at all times. But Miss Moore allowed her the privacy, at least, of shutting the stall door.

She wasn't bad, Miss Moore. She just let things happen. Maybe she wasn't supposed to tell Gwen where Alice was, exactly, maybe that *was* confidential, but she could have told Gwen that Alice was going to be all right, that she was in safe hands.

Gwen thought of a passage Aunt often quoted from the Bible: "He that is not with me is against me: and he that gathereth not with me scattereth." Aunt said that meant that if you didn't help someone when you could, then you were hurting them. Miss Moore hadn't helped when she could.

As Gwen washed her hands at the sink, she could hear the wind blowing harder and wilder through the drafty ward. When the first of the spring storms had come, Gwen had been startled and frightened as she listened to the ghostly moans build into wails in the upper air of the high-ceilinged hallways. She knew, now, that it was only the wind, just like the wind that blew on her face and whipped her hair, this way and that, in the backyard at home.

Looking into the clouded metal mirror above the sink, Gwen saw that her hair was pushed up and tangled; her blouse was creased and its round collar bent. Her eyes were swollen and underlined with shadows. She didn't bother to straighten herself up.

She looked like a crazy lunatic.

Then something in the hazy mirror caught Gwen's

eye; the small bead balls of her key chain were showing from underneath her collar. She looked sideways at Miss Moore. The day nurse was smoothing down the backs of her hands, admiring her shiny nails. Gwen lifted a hand up to her neck and quickly tucked the chain back under the collar of her blouse.

"What time is it?" Gwen asked.

"What? Oh . . ." Miss Moore glanced at her watch. "It's about three thirty."

Four hours they had kept her in the quiet room.

Soon the day shift would be changing over to the evening nurses and attendants. Miss Moore had shed her uniform already; she'd be heading home in half an hour. Gwen dried her hands and followed Miss Moore out through the toilet-room door.

Another bolt of lightning—*BOOM!*—and the rain switched to hail, hitting at the windows like long-nailed fingers, tap-tapping to get inside. Patients paced the hall with their hands over their ears. Gwen saw Janet standing by herself, face to the wall, her arms curled up close to her chest. She looked for Mrs. West but couldn't see her anywhere. The head nurse was probably in the day room telling everyone to occupy themselves until the dinner call, that this was just an ordinary storm, that they were all perfectly safe—

And then she heard it.

Low against the screaming of the wind was the even tone, growing louder and louder, blaring out its urgent and terrifying warning: the air-raid horn!

Gwen watched the crowd of nervous patients milling around the hallway. Didn't they hear it? Gwen could hear it clearly, menacingly, above the clatter of hail. They must get to the tunnel! Why wasn't anyone lining up?

"Should I line up at the stairs, Miss Moore?" Gwen yelled out the words so that the day nurse could hear her above the blaring horn, the wailing air.

"Well, Gwen, you know what Mrs. West said." Miss Moore wasn't even looking at Gwen as she spoke. Her voice was calm, as if nothing was happening, as if she didn't even hear the warning. "Her orders were for you to go to the small activities room. I have to follow . . ."

The last of Miss Moore's words dissolved into the din of anxious girls and women, the blare of the air-raid horn, and the tap-tapping of hail on the windowpanes. Gwen pushed in and out through the groups of patients as she rushed toward the stairwell door. She must get to the tunnel!

Gwen slipped through the door like a mouse through a crack in the wall. Should she have tried to get the others to come? Should she go back and get them, get Janet at least, who might come with her, who was already in the hall?

But she could not turn around. Gwen flew down the stairs, not hearing anyone on the landing above her, just the steady drone of the air-raid horn.

She had to get to the tunnel. Reach the tunnel and she would be safe.

But why weren't the others coming?

An idea came to Gwen in a flash. As she reached the half-floor landing and the door that opened out to the grounds, she hit the metal bar and pushed the outside door wide open. Hail smashed on the landing like shattering glass. Gwen's arms flew up to cover her face. The light on the alarm box smoldered red. Maybe the alarm would alert Mr. Jones, or someone else, to come and help the others on the ward, to get everyone to walk down the stairs quickly.

The wind threw the door shut—*SLAM!*—as Gwen raced down the last half flight of stairs to the basement and the doorway leading into the tunnel.

CHAPTER ELEVEN

Gwen leapt from the last step into the basement of Pineview. The polished floor reflected a single row of fluorescent lights flickering down from the ceiling. A pattern of small stones seemed to swirl through the shiny linoleum and eddy around Gwen's legs; the effect was dizzying. She stood stranded, not knowing what to do.

The basement corridor was crowded with doors. Had there always been so many? The air-raid horn blared in Gwen's ears—she needed to think! She'd been in the basement lots of times, to go to her job at the laundry, for Aunt's visit, and always for the air-raid drills, always through the north tunnel door. She'd never had trouble finding the door before. Why did everything look so strange?

And where were the others?

When the air-raid horn sounded, everyone was supposed to stop what they were doing, the staff, too, and line up by the door. They should be coming down now. Gwen looked up into the stairwell, then back to the basement corridor, searching from door to door. She had to find the way in.

There!

To her left was the sign, the yellow-and-black windmill, the bright letters against a black band: the north tunnel door! Gwen dashed across the corridor and gripped the cold metal handle.

Why weren't the others coming?

Should she run back up the stairs and tell them to hurry, or stay by the tunnel door and wait? The first one down was supposed to hold the tunnel door open for the rest to go through to safety. Gwen always held the door because she was always the first in line, rushed to be first, so she could get down to the basement as quickly as possible.

And here she was, waiting.

But the first one down was the last to go into the tunnel and, once in the tunnel, stood closest to the basement door. Farther into the tunnel seemed safer. Had she been wrong all those times pushing to the front of the line? Some of the women were slow on the stairs. And everyone was slow today. If she wasn't first, she might still be on the stairs when *it happened*.

Gwen's heart leapt to her throat. The blare of the air-raid horn was so irritating! Her hand ached from holding the handle of the door. How long was she going to have to wait?

In the tunnel the girls and women had to stand close together, facing the stacks of water barrels, holding their arms over their heads until the drill was over. Mrs. West said a drill only lasted five minutes, but Gwen's arms would begin to ache the second she lifted them over her head. No one was allowed to lower her arms until the all-clear bell sounded. Hearing the clanging of the bell after a drill was a huge relief. Gwen felt certain that the staff would say it was a drill to avoid panic, even if it was the real thing, a real atom bomb attack.

Suddenly she remembered Alice.

Was someone helping Alice down to a tunnel?

Alice always said that air-raid drills were stupid. When an atom bomb hit, did Gwen really think that putting her hands over her head would make a hoot of difference? They'd still be vaporized instantly. Alice said that when an attack was imminent, the head of the hospital, or the governor, or the president of the United States, should order the staff to unlock every door, unbar every window, let every patient go free for the last few moments before they were all fried to a crisp. Alice said it was only fair for having locked them up for so long.

But what would happen if they did let everyone out and then found that someone had made a mistake, that an atom bomb attack wasn't really under way? Maybe the enemy had changed their minds, or only said they'd fired missiles at the people of the United States of America when they really hadn't. Maybe there had been a big mix-up, and a missile that was supposed to be launched wasn't, that someone had goofed. Then all the patients from the locked wards would be roaming free. How would the staff ever get them back inside? And if the patients didn't get back to their wards, where in the world would they all sleep for the night? What if it started to rain?

Voices from high up in the stairwell broke through Gwen's thoughts. They were finally coming! She knew what she had to do. She would hold the tunnel door. That was the job of the first one down, and she'd been waiting and waiting to do it. But what had taken them so long? It was past five minutes now, long past. The all-clear bell should have sounded minutes ago.

So why hadn't it sounded? Had someone forgotten to stop the drill and sound the all-clear?

Then Gwen knew. The all-clear wasn't going to sound, would never sound again, because *this was not a drill.*

This was a real atom bomb attack.

Could anyone be lucky enough to survive an atom bomb attack *twice*?

Terror rushed through Gwen like a hot wind, like wind on fire, and then, in the next moment, a crashing wave of cold, wet doubt. Had she ever survived an atom bomb attack? Or was it as Dr. Stone had read from her chart, as the brittle headline had spelled out in bold black letters against a yellowing newsprint band?

Couple Die in Fiery Automobile Crash

"*Only child thrown to safety, survives.*" The words formed a whisper in Gwen's mouth. She brought a hand up to her throbbing head, to keep it from lurching to the pulse of the air-raid horn, changed suddenly from its steady drone to a series of urgent, loud blasts—*Honk, honk! Honk, honk! Honk, honk!* Gwen's head felt like it might explode. Had Alice been right, and now they were all going to die?

Mrs. West said that in the tunnel they would be safe.

But Gwen wasn't even in the tunnel!

She tightened her grip on the handle of the door. She was the first one down. She had to wait and hold the door for the others. It was the rule. Gwen's thoughts raced back to the day Aunt had brought her here, when she watched Aunt's eyes fill with tears. This time she couldn't wait for the others. She would not make Aunt cry again.

Gwen pulled.

The metal door slid open. Beyond it was complete darkness. Had the electricity gone out? Gwen couldn't see past the threshold of the tunnel entrance. An active quiet seemed to hold at the open doorway like blue-black water churning behind glass: an ocean of moving quiet. Gwen hesitated, then stepped across the threshold.

"Sink or swim," Alice used to say.

Gwen decided to swim.

The gray slab of the north tunnel door closed shut behind her. The honking of the air-raid horn suddenly stopped; there was no clattering of hail; the voices in the upper stairwell became instantly mute.

Gwen took a step forward. She had to move deeper into the tunnel, but it was so dark that she couldn't see an inch in front of her face. Another step. Her sneakers cracked something underfoot. Other sounds filled in the quiet, not the sounds of patients coming down from the ward, not tunnel sounds at all.

With her next step, the hard floor gave way to something soft and springy.

As Gwen's eyes adjusted, she could make out strange shapes all around her, not the shapes of water barrels but tall, shadowy shapes surrounding her. Something swooped at her face. Her arms flew up to protect her eyes. Gwen peered through the space between her crossed forearms to see what it was and saw it clearly, even though every other thing in the tunnel was vague with darkness. It was the cherry-breasted bird.

A breeze, first heard as a rustle of leaves, blew cool across Gwen's face. She closed her eyes, letting the fresh air stream over her cheeks and eyelids and eddy around the nape of her neck. She had somehow found her way back.

She was in the forest.

The bird fluttered forward, just ahead of Gwen's face. She followed it through the shadows. As they moved, Gwen raised her arms in a flapping motion, like wings, imagining her night eyes as points of stars keeping the small bird within her sight.

After minutes or hours—Gwen had no idea—she began to feel very tired. It must be late. Her outstretched hand brushed against the trunk of a tree. She stopped. A little flutter, and tiny claws pinched as the cherry-breasted bird perched on her shoulder.

Gwen wished she had a flashlight so she could look at the tree. None of the girls had flashlights on the ward. What would they have needed them for, anyway? It wasn't as if they were all at camp! Gwen imagined herself and Alice, and the others, sitting crossed-legged in a circle on the day room floor singing "Oh, Susanna." . . .

The ward. That place seemed long ago and far away.

She held her hand on the tree to mark it in the darkness. Was it the big oak? She wanted it to be. Gwen wrapped her arms around the trunk. Her fingers didn't even come close to meeting at the other side. It could be the oak. She remembered the other time, sitting under its broad branches; the ground had been soft and flat. It would make a good place to lie down.

But the idea of sleeping outside in the forest made Gwen feel not so sleepy anymore. Was she afraid of the dark? No, just not used to it, maybe. Throughout the long months she'd spent on the ward, it had never been really dark. Even at night the halls were brightly lit. Darkness was another thing that had not been allowed.

And she had missed the dark, remembering running through the house on cold, clear nights, turning off all the lights, so that she and Aunt could gaze at the stars.

Were there stars?

Gwen looked way up but could see only shadows. She supposed there could still be stars, but shy ones, hiding behind the leaves of the tree.

There had been a lamppost the other time, too.

Aunt had read aloud a story, once, about a girl who found her way into a forest through a closet full of furs. A single lamppost had lit the girl's way so she wouldn't become lost. Could it be the same for Gwen? She searched the darkness but saw no light, nothing that might help her find her way if she happened to become lost. Her lamppost had had a broken light. And the other was just part of a fairy story.

So what now? Maybe she should try to rest. Probably right where she was would be best. Gwen started to kneel on the ground; then something caught her eye. A faint light projected a smear of yellow onto a patch of dried leaves a short distance away. It seemed to be coming from just around the bend of the tree. Gwen looked for its source and found it, just a little bit of something caught on the trunk of the tree.

A little bit of *light*.

The light was small and yellow, like a flashlight bulb glowing on the outside bark. She looked closer. The light wasn't on the bark; it was coming from inside it.

It was light coming through a keyhole.

Gwen's breath caught on her own thought. She lifted the gold key from around her neck; with a flutter of wings the cherry-breasted bird flew away from her shoulder. Gwen tried the key in the lock. It fit but would not turn. She tried again. The lock seemed rusted stiff. Gwen tried one more time, forcing the key with both hands; there was a sharp *click!* and a door swung out and open.

A rectangle of soft yellow light poured onto the ground, illuminating a scatter of oak leaves, acorns, and pale-green moss. Roots, like heavy guidelines, stretched out from the edge of the doorway, securing it to the shadows. Overhead, the cherry-breasted bird bobbed on a low, leafy branch. And within, there was a little wooden landing and the start of a spiral staircase winding down.

CHAPTER TWELVE

Gwen poked her toe at the landing. It seemed solid enough. She stepped onto it with both feet and jumped. The staircase was as solid as the tree. Gwen peered at the wedge-shaped stairs glowing with yellow light, inviting her to go ahead, *take a step.*

Should she? Maybe she wouldn't have to sleep in the forest after all.

Gwen took a step, then another; she jumped down a few more stairs and stopped. Should she shut the door? Above her the open doorway gaped like a yawning mouth, cavernous against the warm-lit wood. Better to close it, as long as she could open it again from the inside. What if the tree door had an alarm on it like the outside door of Pineview? At least she had the key! Gwen's mouth spread in a wide grin. The muscles on her face weren't used to wide grinning; it felt odd and pleasant, all at the same time.

She walked back up the stairs and looked at the door. There was no metal bar, no electric alarm, no glowing gumdrop light, just an old brass doorknob like the ones at home. Gwen rattled it to check that the latch wasn't rusted stiff or locked on the inside. It wasn't, so she closed the door against the darkness. The barrellike space shut in around her, encircling her with soft light.

Gwen started down the stairs again, letting her hand rub against the close, curved wall of the narrow stairwell. The inner wood felt cool to touch, almost damp, and the wood grain rippled upward in wavy lines. Gwen leaned her head way back. High above her the light funneled into darkness. Looking down, she felt dizzy and sat for a moment on a stair.

The whole staircase seemed carved out of one piece of wood, all the same warm yellow color. Who had carved these stairs, and why were they here? Gwen had no idea at all and let the thought just float away. She stood up, wondering where the staircase ended. The curve in the spiral was so tight that she couldn't see more than a few steps ahead.

Gwen walked down the staircase, step by step, feeling more relaxed than she remembered ever feeling. She'd never been here before, but it seemed familiar somehow, in a comfortable way. Gwen almost expected to find Aunt waiting at the bottom of the stairs with a mug of cocoa and a welcoming hug.

The light inside the tree moved like leaves swaying in

golden air. Maybe it wasn't the air itself that was golden but the air reflecting the yellow-colored wood surrounding it. And that could happen too. Once, last autumn, when all the trees were bright yellow-orange, the leaves had colored the air. The air was orange! Gwen had walked outside with Aunt in the late-afternoon light as if they were strolling in a fairyland. Aunt said she had never seen anything like it in all her years.

"Remember this," she had told Gwen. "It's a gift."

Gwen imagined a gift of orange air wrapped in a nest of autumn leaves. "Remember this," Aunt had said, and she had.

Gwen took a few more steps and found herself at the bottom of the stairs. There was no door, no bars or locks, not even a curtain to draw aside. Another step, and she passed through an open doorway.

She was standing in a small, square room.

A wooden table and a single chair stood directly in front of her. To her right was a tall wooden cupboard with cups and plates set on open shelves. And to her left was an enameled sink with an old water tap. The little room looked just like the square summer kitchen at home, except the floor was pressed dirt, the walls were pressed dirt, and the ceiling, dirt, too, held up by long, bark-stripped branches fanning out from the open doorway. Roots, probably. It was a little kitchen dug under the forest, deep under the brown earth, an earth kitchen.

"Hello?"

Gwen's voice poked at the quiet in the room.

"Is anyone home?"

She asked, but felt she knew the answer already. There was no one at home but Gwen.

A thin layer of dirt coated the surface of the table; patches of brass showed through the chrome on the water tap. Wisps of a spider's web hung from the ceiling roots, but even that looked abandoned. No one had been at home here for a very long time. And how could someone have come in anyway? Gwen had the key.

She walked up to the table, placing her open hands on the surface. The wood felt cool, like the curved wall of the staircase, like a living thing: alive.

Gwen looked past the table. In the far corner was her bed. The light-and-dark patterns of her quilt spread over the white sheets, and over that lay her nightgown, a soft, cream-colored lawn scattered with pink rosettes. Draped on a chair by the foot of the bed was her summer robe with dirt stains on the knees, still visible from where she had knelt in the garden to do something or other; she couldn't remember exactly what. It didn't seem important now. On the nightstand by her bed was a lamp with a dotted milk-glass base. It glowed faintly, as if by candle-light, and next to the lamp was a glass of water.

Gwen pulled off her sneakers and socks, her dungarees and blouse, and slipped the soft nightgown over her
head; its overlong hem gathered on the dirt floor. She
crawled into bed, bunching the white sheet to her nose to
breathe in the *whoosh* of hot steam, the plain and pat-
terned squares, the overwhelming ease of sleep.

Even before Gwen opened her eyes, she could smell
the moist earth surrounding her and sense the quiet as if
it were another person in the room. She opened her eyes.
There were her clothes, just as she had left them on the
chair at the foot of the bed, her quilt and nightstand, and
all around her the little dirt room. Her stomach growled.
She was hungry! Maybe there was food to eat in the
kitchen?

Gwen hadn't looked around much last night, but she
had seen a cupboard. She supposed she could hardly
hope to find something still worth eating in there. Food
left to sit for a long time became spoiled, or rock hard,
or half eaten by mice. Once a mouse had eaten through
the cardboard of the oatmeal box and moved inside,
munching and munching on the flattened grain. When
Gwen had gone to pour out some oatmeal, out tumbled
a clump of pale pink mouse babies, oatmeal flakes sticking to the gray bumps of their unopened eyes. She
remembered their little legs squirming for their lost nest.

But that hadn't happened in this kitchen. It was some-where else that she couldn't recall.

Oatmeal would taste good right now, with brown sugar, and a chunk of butter melted on the top. Scram-bled eggs and toast would taste good, too. Gwen put on her robe and walked over to the sink. Turning the faucet on, she placed her hands under the cool water, splashing it over her face and arms. There wasn't a towel, so she wiped herself dry with her sleeve.

Back at her bed, Gwen pulled the top sheet and quilt up over her pillow, smoothing it all down. On her chair was a green gingham blouse, neatly folded. Was that the blouse she'd worn yesterday? Gwen held it up, consider-ing the question for a moment, then shrugged and got dressed.

Now to look for food.

The cupboard was over on the far wall. If there wasn't any food in there, then she'd have to try her luck up in the forest. She didn't know very much about finding food in a forest, only that some wild plants were poisonous—which ones were safe to eat, she really didn't know.

But as Gwen passed by the wooden table, a tray of food appeared. First it wasn't there, and then it was. In the wells of the tray were scrambled eggs and hash browns, three sausage links, and toast. In the one round well was a small glass of orange juice with a white paper cap on top. She was hungry, and here was food! Gwen sat down and started to eat.

As she chewed on a piece of toast, Gwen looked around the small dirt room. There was light in the earth kitchen, much brighter than last night, but no windows or an overhead lamp. How was that possible? She finished her orange juice and carried her tray to the faucet to rinse it. As she placed it in the sink, the tray and fork and spoon and cup simply disappeared.

Gwen thought for a moment. Should she concern herself with these appearances and disappearances? Then she wondered why any of it needed wondering. She walked over to the cupboard.

The cupboard was made of the same warm-colored wood as the table. It had double doors at the bottom and, above them, a drawer with a single knob. Above the drawer were open shelves filled with things. On the first deep shelf was a pile of yellowed newspapers and magazines. The next two shelves held stacks of plates and cups, odd pieces in different patterns; on the top of one stack was a china teacup, blue and white.

On the highest shelf of the cupboard was a bundle of pressed white towels. Gwen lifted one down. The cloth unfolded in her hand as she brought it to her face, breathing in the smell of steam. Her hands refolded the towel as if she'd done the motion a hundred times—*flat from the sheet press, folded in thirds, then folded in half so the selvage didn't show.* Gwen tucked the folded white cloth under her arm.

On the dirt wall, at right angles to the cupboard, hung a large framed picture. It looked like some kind of map. Gwen lifted the frame off the wall and carried the heavy picture over to the table, where the light was better. She carefully laid it down.

The glass was coated with particles of fine dust. There were small bubbles and imperfections in the large pane; it must be very old. Old glass had bubbles and rippled streaks; new glass was clear and smooth and embedded with thin wire mesh. Gwen paused for a moment. Now why would she think a thing like that? She shook the thought out of her head as briskly as she shook out the white towel; she wiped the surface of the old glass clean.

Gwen peered at the picture in the frame. It was a map of a garden, with the words *The Garden* written in fancy letters and curlicues along the bottom. The garden was in the shape of a square, and the large, square garden was divided by paths into four equally square flower beds. And growing in the very center of the garden was a large tree. A wall ran along the outside border of the garden, close to the map edge.

Near the top of the map, at the end of the top path, was a fancy letter *N* for North, with an arrow pointing upward. Gwen had seen this feature on other maps, always the arrow pointing north, but the drawing of this 𝒩 with its arrow was so fine that the arrow itself seemed real, like something she could hold in her hand: a compass point quivering on a pin.

And above the 𝒩 and the arrow, at the northernmost point of the garden map, was a simple iron gate.

Gwen's breath caught in her chest; her heart beat quickly, one, two beats. She turned her eyes away from the top of the drawing, away from the iron gate. Picking up the smudged white towel, she draped it over the upper edge of the map, lifted up the top of the frame, and anchored the rest of the towel securely in place underneath the weight of glass and wood. Gwen drew in a deep breath and slowly let it out; she turned back to look at the map.

The more Gwen looked, the more she saw. The four square flower beds surrounding the central tree were really groups of smaller flower beds, interconnected with gravel paths. Each of these smaller beds was drawn with pencil and dabbed with watercolor to show the kinds of flowers planted there, with the names of the flowers written in cursive. They had strange-sounding names like *Alcea rosea*, *Tropaeolum*, *Delphinium*, and *Ruta*: flower names that poked like shoots of fresh color through a mat of dark-brown earth.

She wanted to live in this garden. The soft green leaves on the large tree were so sparkly, so lifelike, they seemed to sway as if in a breeze. Oak leaves. The gravel paths wandered through the garden like riverbeds of multicolored stone. And on one of the paths, drawn close to the big oak, was a tall, plain post.

Gwen looked closer.

No, not a post, but a lamppost. It was painted a deep forest green, with four clear panes of glass for the lamp. Gwen felt a strange sensation around her eyes; her vision blurred.

The garden was above her.

But it wasn't a garden anymore. Only the large oak tree remained, and a rusted lamppost that could give no light.

Gwen lifted up the heavy picture frame and turned it over on the table; the white covering cloth slipped to the floor. Small nails held the map and glass in place. First with her fingers, then pulling the chain over her head and using the edge of her gold key, Gwen pried out the nails and pulled off the board backing. The map ruffed out of its frame.

She had to know for sure.

Gwen rolled up the map to carry it, grabbed her gold key, and ran up the spiral staircase and out the oak tree door.

. . .

Whitish daylight leached through the overhanging leaves and onto the surface of the map. Now, where was the lamppost she'd found the other time?

Gwen glanced over her shoulder, and there it was, broken, paint peeling, just as she'd remembered it from before.

If this was the garden in the drawing, then somewhere buried underneath her feet were the gravel paths. Gwen checked the map and started digging, pushing with a stick into the soft soil until it hit something hard. She dropped to her knees and started digging with her hands, lifting out clods of dirt and mats of rotted oak leaves. An acorn appeared, lidless and hollow; it broke apart in Gwen's hand. She dug deeper, stretching her full arms' length to lift out the last clumps of leaves and dirt. Gwen straightened and stood up; below her the multicolored stones were exposed.

She peered into the hole at the long-ago garden path.

A sheen came off the gravel, shiny, as if it were polished or wet. The random patterns of the small stones swirled like moving water, beckoning Gwen to jump in. She did. Her sneakers met the exposed path with a suctionlike grip.

Gwen stood in the thigh-deep hole looking out, trying to imagine the paths, the flowers and lit lamp, the soft noises of a garden surrounding her. But she could not. Even the gravel wasn't right anymore; it had fused together, become smooth underfoot: unkickable.

Crawling out, Gwen pushed the dirt and blackish leaves back into the useless hole. She stamped and stamped on the raised mound to smash it down, to bury the too-smooth gravel that would never be a garden path again. Gwen felt dirty, covered with the clinging slips of leaves.

She sat down in a heap of damp and stayed there for a long while.

A rustle in the branches of the old oak caused Gwen to look up. Overhead, on the narrow end of a limb, swayed the cherry-breasted bird. It cocked its head as if it were looking at her with its black bead eyes.

Gwen pushed herself up from the ground. She brushed off the larger clumps of leaves and dirt, rolled up the map, and walked down the narrow staircase to the earth kitchen.

On the table in front of her single chair was a dinner on a tray; Gwen sat down and ate. After she finished, the tray disappeared. Lying on the table next to where the tray had been was a white envelope addressed in blue-black ink:

Miss Gwendolyn Brace

Gwen didn't read the rest of the address. She picked up the letter between her finger and thumb, and walked it over to the cupboard. Reaching up, she laid the white envelope, unopened, on the top shelf.

On the lowest shelf of the cupboard was the stack of old newspapers and magazines. The top, bold headline caught her eye:

U.S. Ready for Nuclear Showdown, President Grave: Asserts Hemisphere in Great Danger

Gwen flipped the newspaper over so the headline was no longer visible, then walked back to the table, unrolled the map, and smoothed it out flat. Her eyes surveyed the smaller garden beds within the larger square plots, noting the precise locations of the flowers with their unpronounceable flower names.

She dug her hand into her dungaree pocket, looking for something. It was still there, the twig with the three acorns. She needed the twig. Gwen twisted the acorns off the stem. For a moment she held the polished nuts in her hand; they felt weightless, without mass.

Gwen brought the top newspaper over to the table. All she needed was string. Maybe she could make string from a strip of paper, twisting it until it was strong enough. She opened the newspaper to an inside page, ripped a long, thin strip from the yellowed edge, and twisted it into a paper cord. That would work.

Turning back to the front page, Gwen ripped off the wide, dark headline. She bunched and wrapped the strip of newsprint around and around the top of the twig, then tied it in place with the paper string.

Holding the twig in her hand, Gwen smiled. The headline was no longer readable, and now it was something pretty, a pretty paper flower.

That was one.

Gwen took the blue-and-white teacup down from the cupboard shelf, set it on the table, and placed the flower in the cup. It looked nice. What she needed now were more twigs; she could find those in the forest. She already had a lot of paper.

Gwen looked closely at the garden map. It would take a lot of work, but she knew she could do it.

She'd start first thing in the morning.

CHAPTER THIRTEEN

Gwen needed more flowers. She hadn't made nearly enough. Three times she'd gone out for more twigs, but now the newspaper was running out. She carried a bundle of paper flowers up to the forest, checked the map, and pushed each flower into the dirt where a real flower might have bloomed. It was going to be a big job. Really big.

Taking her bearings from the old oak, Gwen planted the last of the paper flowers she had made; she stood back and looked around her. She'd have to start using the magazines. Gwen went to collect more twigs.

One afternoon Gwen came down for lunch to find a stack of colored paper, a pair of blunt-nosed scissors, string, a pencil, and a bag of smooth blond sticks sitting on the wooden table. She couldn't believe her luck! She'd worked through the back cover of the last magazine in the pile and had been wondering all morning how she could continue to make the paper flowers when all the paper was used up. Making them from dried leaves, her only other idea, just wouldn't have given the right effect.

But the colored paper!

Gwen rubbed her hand over the stack of red and orange and yellow and blue sheets. She picked up the ball of string; no having to make string from paper anymore. And a pencil and scissors! Now she could draw different petal shapes and cut them out straight. Gwen sat down and started making a flower with the top, red sheet.

Things appeared in the earth kitchen, but she never concerned herself too much about it. She had what she needed, didn't she? And what she didn't have showed up. That was just the way it was.

Gwen finished making an armload of colored-paper flowers by early evening and planted them among the newspaper and magazine flowers. The effect was quite pretty. Still, she needed more. She looked again at the garden map, checking the curves of the smaller beds, the square corners of the four large sections: how the garden had been, once upon a time, when it was alive.

The paper kept appearing, and other supplies, too, whenever she needed more. And every evening, before going to bed, Gwen put the paper and scissors, the pencil and sticks and string, back on the lowest cupboard shelf. On the top shelf a stack of white envelopes grew. Each time one appeared, she placed it, unopened, on top of the others.

Gwen could tell she was getting nearer her goal as she took each new armful of paper flowers up to the forest. The air was changing. It was chilly in the evenings, and the mornings, too. And the hours of daylight grew less and less.

She had woken up one morning not too long ago to find her summer robe replaced with a plaid flannel one draped on the chair. She'd slipped the roomy navy-and-green robe over her shoulders and brought the wide lapels up to her nose, breathing in. The flannel smelled of new cloth, and something else. Gwen buried her face in the soft folds and breathed again. It smelled of *something*. Something nice. But she couldn't seem to get her thoughts around exactly what.

A new cardigan and undershirt had appeared that same morning in the pile of folded clothes at the foot of her bed. Autumn must be coming on, though she'd never bothered counting the days.

Planting the last flower from an armful of paper flowers, Gwen realized that she'd done it. The flower beds, abandoned such a long time ago, were now in full bloom. She'd even tied paper flowers to the limbs of a few of the smaller trees to give the effect of flowering shrubs.

Gwen turned, looking all around her paper garden. A little wind picked up, lifting her bangs away from her forehead. The colored-paper petals, the magazine and newspaper petals, slapped in the breeze like holiday bunting, tied on their rigid stick stems. Had she really believed that the garden would come to life? No. Not really. But she had hoped the flowers might sway. Her garden was made of paper and sticks, not living flowers that grew and bloomed and swayed. There wasn't even any scent.

It was just a paper garden.

Gwen turned away. She didn't want to look anymore.

Down in the earth kitchen it was quiet. The paper-flower-making supplies lay spread out across the wooden table. In the middle of the table, the first paper flower Gwen had made sat on show in its china teacup. There was a chip on the cup edge that she hadn't noticed before; a threadlike crack that ran from the cup lip down through the blue-and-white china. It was a teacup that could hold no water; just right for a paper flower that would never need any.

The garden map lay on the table too. A paper map of a paper garden.

Gwen felt suddenly flat, without dimension.

She cast a glance around the earth kitchen, floating a thought out into the quiet—something on her mind that she hadn't had time to think about before.

Her eyes focused on the wooden cupboard.

She had been looking for something. . . .

Gwen knelt down in front of the cupboard and pulled the double doors open. Inside were a tulip vase, some remnants of calico-patterned material, and a green-enameled tin. Gwen picked up the tin; something inside *clunked*.

She looked up and found herself face-to-face with the cupboard drawer, her nose and the drawer knob just inches apart. Above the knob was a keyhole cut into the wood. She hadn't noticed the keyhole before. Gwen pulled herself up and gave the knob a tug. The drawer was locked.

Gwen lifted the metal-bead chain from around her neck and held the gold key. But it changed in her hand. It wasn't her gold key.

For a moment, it was a dull-gray *tin* key.

Then it turned back again into gold. Gwen fit the gold key into the keyhole.

One turn, *click!* and the cupboard drawer slid open. Inside the drawer was her witch's hat. What was that doing here?

The thin black gauze looked flimsy; teardrops of

hardened glue held the strands of orange yarn hair in a half-moon along the inside of the brim. But she hadn't found it in the drawer. She was getting the order mixed up.

"Gwen?"

What was that? Gwen's fingers stretched and grabbed at a sound darting like an echo around the little room, the bed, the table, the cupboard, the stairs.

Her eyes shot outward, aiming at the open doorway.

. . . and if you try to come in . . .

Gwen held the thought for a moment. Would someone try? She lowered her eyes and turned back to the open cupboard drawer.

She had the key. No one would *dare* to come in.

Gwen lifted out the witch's hat and put it on her head. The brim slipped down over her eyes, and the hair hung all wrong. She pushed the hat away from her face; it tipped backward and fell to the dirt floor. She just left it there. It had never fit her very well.

There had been something else.

Lying in the bottom of the cupboard drawer was a manila envelope. Gwen pulled it out and pried up the silvery prongs holding the paper flap closed. Inside was a stack of yellowed newspaper clippings, like a bundle of fall leaves. Gwen slid them out onto the table.

She had been looking for something, and she had found it.

Letters, typeset into words, laid out in paper columns telling a sad story; bold headlines arranged to grab and alarm—how could words on paper hurt like this?

Gwen faced the paper words, face-to-typeface.

Suddenly she knew.

The last clipping in the pile was just a yellowed photograph. A thick black line formed a box around the outer edge. The caption read, simply: *Recent photograph.* It was a picture of a man and woman, smiling. In front of the couple stood a young girl, a twig in her hand, gazing steadily out at the camera.

The three were posed by the trunk of a sprawling tree in front of a clapboard house. On the left of the photograph was a lamppost with house numbers hanging off to one side on a horizontal pole. On either side of the photograph, running along the lower edge, was a wooden fence. And along the fence, and spilling into the yard, was a profusion of flowers: hollyhocks, nasturtiums, larkspur, rue. The photograph, taken from outside the fence, framed the three through the opened gate.

Tears pricked the surface of the brittle newsprint, falling from Gwen's eyes.

With trembling hands Gwen picked up the first newspaper clipping and bunched and wrapped the strip of paper words around and around a blond stick, tying the newspaper in place with a length of string. She picked up the next clipping and the next, setting each finished paper flower in the blue-and-white cup. Finally, she propped the newspaper photo of the happy family up against the bouquet of paper flowers in the teacup vase, covering over the chip.

Gwen gathered the rest of the flower-making supplies into a pile and laid the pile in the empty cupboard drawer. She pushed the drawer shut.

After breakfast the next morning, Gwen found a white envelope on the table by her tray. It was the same as the others, maybe a bit thicker. She picked it up and opened it, slipping the white paper out of its sleeve.

Gwen held the folded sheets in her hand. Tucked in the center crease was a bouquet of pressed flowers, papery tissue now, their moisture and brilliance pressed away with only a silhouette connecting each flattened shape to something that had been alive. The pressed flowers seemed to float on top of the even waves of blue-black ink like petals on a rough sea, the letters cresting in *f*s and *l*s and *t*s: Aunt's handwriting.

She remembered Aunt.

Gwen tipped the pressed flowers into her roughened hand. They felt like nothing at all. One breath and the petals, stems, and leaves blew in a scatter across the garden map. She turned to read the letter in her hand.

Dearest Gwennie, How's my girl? . . .

After she finished, Gwen folded the letter and brushed the pressed flowers into the nest of words, sliding the folded paper back into its envelope. Then she slipped the last page of the letter out again. In the space below the words *from your loving Aunt* was a pencil sketch: a simple outline of the new flower beds Aunt had tilled for next year. *We'll plant them together,* Aunt had written.

It was time.

Gwen carried the wooden frame, the sheet of glass, and the cardboard backing over to the table and put the map back into its frame; she pushed the small nails that held everything in place into the inner sides of the soft wood with the flat of her scissors. Then she hung the map back on its hook. Gwen looked around the room at the tall cupboard, the enameled sink, and the wooden table and chair. Everything was in order.

What about her key?

She'd have to leave it behind, and the paper flowers, too. She could take none of that with her. Then she remembered the letters.

Gwen lifted down the stack of Aunt's letters from the cupboard shelf. Was that all? She walked to the doorway and turned, looking all around the brown earth kitchen.

Her eyes rested on her own neatly made bed. Her quilt. She mustn't forget that. Gwen went over to the bed and folded the quilt into a bundle, setting the letters on top.

Then she walked to the open doorway and started up the stairs. Halfway up, Gwen stopped and rested her cheek against the cool, moist wood of the inner bark. With her ear so close, she could hear a soft murmur, like the sound of a stream, flowing, flowing. She continued to climb, listening to the rustle of wind through the leaves of the large oak tree.

Gwen opened the door and stepped out into the paper garden. The air had a sharpness to it. She paused for just a moment, then closed the heavy oak door shut. Looking up into the canopy of leaves, Gwen noticed tips of yellow-orange beginning to spread over the dark green, with cracks of cobalt sky beyond. In the crook of a branch the cherry-breasted bird had settled in to roost, its bead eyes watching her.

There would be a frost soon.

Gwen set her quilt and the letters on the ground and lifted the gold key over her head; the three tiny oak leaves fanned out from its handle and the acorns clustered beneath, all carved in the precious metal. She laid the key on a patch of moss at the base of the tree, then stood and wrapped her arms around the big oak. Dr. Stone had felt like this, she remembered, and smiled.

She picked up her things and walked up the path, heading north, to the iron gate.

As Gwen touched the gate, she sensed a change in the air. She looked back. The paper flowers seemed softer in color; a single light appeared in the distance. Turning again to the gate, Gwen felt the ground crunch under her shoes, a sensation of small stones shifting. Then she pushed the gate open and walked through. Iron hinges swung silently shut as the gate closed behind her.

Gwen walked forward along the path, and the noise of the ward flooded in: the squeaking of her sneakers on the linoleum floor; the shuffling feet of the other patients on the ward; the active sounds of people all around her. First the noise; then she began to see where she was, like a mist rising. What she saw confused her greatly.

In front of her, to the sides, on the tables in the day room, the chairs, in the hall, on every possible surface, were the paper flowers.

CHAPTER FOURTEEN

"In or out, please." The voice came from behind Gwen.

"What?" Her mouth felt dry and woolly.

"No standing in the doorway. In or out, please." It was the day room nurse.

Gwen stepped out into the hallway. A woman patient hurried past, bumping Gwen's shoulder; she drew her arms in close. She was standing by the ward bulletin board. Newsprint and colored paper flowers surrounded its wooden frame like a garland. On a bright-orange paper background, a sign with slip-in cards read:

Today is WEDNESDAY, OCTOBER 9, 1963.
It is a COOL AND SUNNY day.

October? How long had she been away?

Gwen looked at the ward as if she were seeing it for the first time. The paper flowers filled the hallway like a garden in full bloom. They were pretty, even cheerful, but—Gwen searched for the word and found it—the ward looked *shabby*. The sky-blue paint on the walls in the hallway curled away from the plaster at the ceiling's edge.

Seamlike cracks spread through the old linoleum, matching the cracks in the plank floor underneath. Gwen bent down and rubbed her finger over a raised nailhead working its way out of the wood. She was surprised she hadn't noticed it all before. The walls, the floor, the chairs, and the tables—everything was peeling or cracked or pockmarked with use.

Gwen felt a dull longing for the place she'd left behind. She could remember a garden—not a living, growing garden, but a paper garden made with paper flowers just like the ones on the ward. She tried to stitch together a picture of it in her mind, but it seemed more picture now than real: a picture in a photograph album. And there had been somewhere else, stairs leading down; Gwen shook her head, and the thought just fell away.

A linen cart rattled down the hallway, pushed by one of the ward attendants. Someone was yelling in the day room; a nurse Gwen didn't recognize hurried from the nurses' station and through the day room door.

Gwen felt dizzy; maybe she should find somewhere quiet and sit down. She walked into the girls' sleeping room and over to her sleeping area; she sat on the edge of the bed. Her quilt was still folded in her arms, along with the bundle of letters from Aunt. Gwen laid them down on the smooth white sheet.

Everything was just as she had left it, except for one

thing. On her nightstand was an empty coffee can filled with paper flowers. Gwen reached out and rubbed a blue-paper petal between her finger and thumb.

Looking out the window, she could clearly see changes in the season. Autumn was coming on. The oak leaves on the tree outside her sleeping-room window were turning yellow-orange at their tips. Even the color of the sky was different: a deep, deep blue.

Changes everywhere.

Gwen looked at the bed next to hers. It was made up with white sheets from the laundry and a gray hospital blanket. On the chair by the foot of the bed was a hospital robe; it looked smallish, the size that might fit any one of the girls, a girl who had no robe of her own.

She remembered Alice.

Sadness rushed through Gwen like a cold wind. She pulled her cardigan close around her. Alice was gone.

Gwen lifted the bunch of paper flowers out of the coffee can and carried them over to Alice's old sleeping area, to the bed Alice used to sleep in, and the pillow she tossed at Gwen every single morning when they were together on the ward. It wasn't Alice's bed anymore, Gwen knew that, but she laid the paper flowers on the pillow anyway. They looked nice. She tried to fix Alice's face in her mind, her hollow cheeks and tired eyes, but also her smile; when Alice smiled, her eyes sparkled.

She sat on the side of the bed that used to be Alice's bed, picked up one of the paper flowers, and tossed it back at her own pillow. She tossed another flower, and another, remembering Alice, who never missed a chance to throw something at Gwen in the morning. A wide grin spread across Gwen's face, wet with tears. That's what she loved best about Alice; Alice could always make her smile.

Gwen wiped her face and walked over to her own bed. She picked up the flowers from her pillow, and the ones that had fallen on the floor, and put them back in the coffee can. She unfolded her quilt and spread it over the top sheet. Her navy-and-green robe was draped on the wooden chair at the foot of her bed. And her nightgown was folded between her pillow and the top sheet, under the smoothed-out quilt.

Gwen sat eating her breakfast in the dining hall with the other girls on the ward. As she finished, Mrs. Libby came up.

"Gwen, honey, how are you?"

"Good, thanks." Gwen smiled.

Mrs. Libby put her hand on Gwen's back and gave it a little rub. It felt nice.

"Okay girls, finish up," Mrs. Libby said. She leaned over to Gwen. "You wait with me, hon. Dr. Stone wants to see you in his office this morning."

Gwen didn't mind seeing Dr. Stone.

As she and Mrs. Libby walked out of Pineview and into the crisp morning air, Gwen remembered the other time they had walked that way together. It had been a warm June morning, and she was hoping to go home. Gwen could hardly account for the time gone by. She wrestled with the words that explained what had happened, but her thoughts kept jumping all over the place. Maybe she should ask Dr. Stone?

"Gwen, come in!" Dr. Stone's voice boomed from his doorway into the secretary's office.

Gwen's eyes lingered on the large bouquet of paper flowers in an opal-glass vase on Miss Avery's desk. Turning to Dr. Stone, she observed that nothing had changed about him. He was still the same Dr. Stone, all the way up to his crooked bow tie.

"Miss Avery, hold my calls."

Dr. Stone closed the office door behind them and beckoned for Gwen to sit down. On his desk, and tucked into gaps on the large bookshelf behind it, were pencil holders filled with paper flowers. She had been right about one thing: Dr. Stone was the type to have a messy desk, and a messy office, too. His desk was covered not just with the paper flowers, but with all sorts of other papers. And his shelves were stuffed with books pushed in every which way. Gwen smiled, thinking of Dr. Stone fumbling around trying to find the things he needed. She looked up to see him watching her, his eyebrows raised.

"You have a messy office," Gwen began. "I thought you might."

"Oh, you did, did you?" Dr. Stone was smiling, too. "Well, I'm afraid it's true. And the worst of it is, I lose things all the time! But the flowers cheer things up, don't you think?"

Gwen looked at Dr. Stone carefully. His eyes met hers, and his expression changed.

"So you've decided to come back to us, Gwen. That's good, very good. I'm very glad indeed."

Had she really been away?

"Dr. Stone," Gwen started, "I know I was gone, and I know what I see . . ." She nodded toward the paper flowers on Dr. Stone's desk. "But . . ." She became quiet. Everywhere she looked, on the ward, in Miss Avery's office and Dr. Stone's, even in the dining hall, were the paper flowers.

"Gwen . . ." Dr. Stone paused, seeming to change his mind.

Time for the little cuckoo to chirp again.

"Gwen, I want you to listen closely to what I have to say." He took in a deep breath and let it out. "You needed a safe place, and I think you found one. Healing takes time, Gwen, sometimes a very long time. A number of months have gone by. Did you know that?"

She nodded.

"But the important thing, the most important thing, is that you found your way back to us."

Yes, she had.

"Do you mind answering a few questions, Gwen?"

She shook her head. She didn't mind.

"First, can you tell me today's full date?"

"It's, um, October 10, 1963. A Thursday."

"Yes, that's absolutely right. That was the easy question." Dr. Stone met her eyes. "Now I want you to think back to a year ago. Before you came to the hospital. Can you remember back to that time?"

She remembered.

"Can you tell me what you think happened to cause your aunt to bring you here to the hospital?"

Gwen thought for a moment. It was after the Halloween party.

"Dr. Davis told Aunt that it might be best for me to come here. He's our family doctor back home."

"And what do you think prompted Dr. Davis to recommend that to your aunt? Take your time, Gwen, and really think."

She should be able to answer this.

"I remember I couldn't sleep very well, and Aunt was

worried. Something had happened at school during the Halloween party. I had to take my witch's hat off during the air-raid drill." Gwen paused for a moment. "Mrs. Perry, my teacher, sent a note home to Aunt. I didn't want to go to school anymore."

Why hadn't she wanted to go to school? *Think!*

"I was afraid that if . . ." Was it okay to say that? Gwen looked up into Dr. Stone's eyes. She was safe here. She had to tell him.

"I was afraid that I might be at school during an atom bomb attack." And what? There was more. What had she been afraid of?

"I wouldn't go to school. I said I was sick so I could stay home with Aunt. There was going to be a real attack. I read it in the newspapers. Aunt put the papers away, but I found them and read them. When the newspapers said the danger was over, I thought they just wrote that to get me to go back to school, away from Aunt."

And then they would drop the Bomb and separate her from Aunt, forever.

Aunt had taken Gwen to see Dr. Davis. He said she wasn't sick, not like a cold, or influenza, nothing like that. How did Aunt put it? Gwen was frightened in her mind, and the hospital would help her learn to feel not so frightened anymore, so she could come home and want to go to school again, want to be with the other children.

"I was afraid I might be separated from Aunt, that I might lose her, too, like I lost my parents, that an atom bomb would explode and kill Aunt, just like it happened with my mother and father. But . . ."

She had been looking for her witch's hat on the morning of the party, gone out to the summer kitchen to look, and found it and the tin of old keys in the bottom of the storage cupboard. She had tried a key and opened the locked drawer.

Gwen looked up and met Dr. Stone's gaze.

"But my parents weren't killed in an atom bomb explosion. They died in an automobile accident. And I didn't."

Suddenly, there was nothing more to say. Gwen felt hollow, completely empty, as if someone had drained all the cardboard barrels in the tunnel, and the stale gray water had just poured away to nothing.

Gwen sat staring at her hands folded in her lap. Dr. Stone sat, too. She had something she needed to ask.

She looked up at Dr. Stone.

"Will I ever go away again?" She wanted to be back for good. She wanted to go home to Aunt and stay there.

Dr. Stone rested his chin on his clasped hands, his expression seeming to move like gears and pulleys, turning and tugging in his head.

"Gwen," he began, "the truth is we can't know for

certain. I hope and believe you won't need to leave us again. Not in the way you are asking."

She wanted to believe it too.

"I want to keep you in Pineview for a few more weeks, for observation, and to give you a little more time to adjust to being back with us. And I'd like to put you on garden group. They're preparing the flower beds for winter and could use a hand. A good dose of fresh air might be just the thing to blow all the cobwebs away." He smiled at Gwen. "Does that sound all right to you?"

She nodded. She wanted to be on garden group, but—

"And then, Gwen, if all goes well, I want to send you home. I'll call your aunt this afternoon to tell her about our plans."

Gwen leapt out of her chair and put her arms around Dr. Stone. Hugging his broad chest felt just like hugging the old oak tree in the front yard at home.

Home.

"Any more questions, Gwen?" Dr. Stone asked, half chuckling.

Gwen shook her head but wouldn't let go. She hugged and hugged Dr. Stone.

CHAPTER FIFTEEN

It was midmorning, and Gwen's suitcase was packed. In it were her summer and winter clothes, the large bundle of letters Aunt had sent to her over the long months, and a bouquet of paper flowers, pressed flat for packing. A new day nurse, Miss Allen, had helped Gwen make her quilt into a bundle with a string handle, so she could carry it more easily. Miss Moore didn't work on the ward anymore—"given the sack" was what a woman patient had said. But Gwen wondered if Miss Moore had just woken up one morning and couldn't be bothered to put on her nurse's uniform and show up.

Gwen sat on the edge of her bed and rubbed her hand across the smooth white sheets. It would be some other girl's bed soon. New sheets, new blanket. That was fine with Gwen. She was wearing her coat from last winter. The weather had turned cold over the past week, and yesterday there had been a frost. The coat was small on her, and the cuffs of her blouse showed below the heavy woolen sleeves. She picked up her suitcase and quilt and walked out of the sleeping room.

Mary and Janet were standing in the hall. Gwen had said good-bye to the others earlier that morning.

"Good-bye, Mary. Good-bye, Janet." Gwen tried to shake hands, but Mary pulled away. Janet started to cry. "I promise I'll write."

Mrs. West stood in front of the nurses' station.

"Good-bye, Gwendolyn. The staff and I wish you every success in life." Mrs. West said it as if she actually meant it.

"Good-bye." Gwen waved her hand at the ward that had been her home for almost a year. Quickly, she reached out and hugged Mrs. West. The head nurse stiffened, but Gwen held on for another moment. Mrs. West patted Gwen's back awkwardly.

"Time to go, now, Gwendolyn. That's a good girl."

Gwen let go. She watched Mrs. West carefully smooth down her white nurse's uniform and straighten her cap.

Then Gwen followed Miss Allen down the stairs and into the basement of Pineview. The day nurse opened the door, and they walked into the north tunnel lined with the barrels of water. But there was something new. Large wooden crates with the same "CD" stamped in yellow on the sides were stacked in rows on top of the barrels. Gwen hadn't seen the crates before.

"Miss Allen?" The day nurse turned to look back at

Gwen. "What's in those wooden boxes?"

"What's that? Oh, the boxes. They're the new fallout shelter rations."

"What's *in* the boxes, exactly? Do you know?"

"In the boxes? Oh, crackers and hard candy. Food, you know, in case of an air raid. The Civil Defense officer said it will keep for at least twenty years." The nurse looked down at Gwen, smiling. "Why do you ask?"

She shrugged her shoulders. She just wanted to know. Water and crackers and hard candy: food for the survivors of an atom bomb attack. Gwen remembered Alice's lunatics and murderers, just people really, patients like Alice and herself. No patient would have thought up something as crazy as that.

Gwen and the day nurse came to the end of the tunnel and walked down the corridor toward the lobby of the Main Building. They passed the Records Office door. The reception desk was up ahead; on the edge of the wooden desktop was a vase full of colorful paper flowers.

As they turned from the hall into the visitors' lounge, there was Aunt.

Gwen dropped her suitcase and quilt.

"Aunt!"

Gwen buried her face in Aunt's soft shoulder; she smelled like coffee and clothes off the line and the wool of her navy-blue going-out coat. Aunt's arms wrapped around Gwen, too, like a hundred warm quilts tucked in just right. Gwen nestled her cheek into the crook of Aunt's arm, when—*Honk!*

It was the start-up blare of the air-raid horn.

Gwen's heart leapt to her throat. Her eyes raced up to see Aunt looking toward the day nurse, a startled expression on her face.

"An air-raid drill, Mrs. Jewel," Miss Allen said, speaking loudly over the noise, "for the patients and staff on the open wards. Visitors are not required to participate." The nurse turned to Gwen, almost yelling. "You don't need to participate, either. You're no longer a patient here." She smiled in Gwen's direction.

Gwen clung to Aunt, then realized that she couldn't pick up her suitcase and bundle and hold on to Aunt at the same time. Reluctantly she let go, picked up her things, and turned her mouth close to Aunt's ear.

"I want to go home."

Gwen walked with Aunt out through the large oak door of the main entrance into a gray October morning. The ward bulletin board had posted the weather for today as "cloudy; chance of snow flurries." Gwen hoped it might snow; new snow was like a crisp, clean sheet smoothed over the cold world, quiet and safe. The heavy oak door swung back on its frame, muffling the sound of the air-raid horn to almost no sound at all. They walked down the wide stone steps to a waiting taxi.

As the taxi pulled away from the front circle of the Unity State Hospital, Gwen turned in her seat next to Aunt to look back at the red-brick buildings falling farther and farther into the distance. They drove through the open iron gate, and Gwen watched until the hospital was just a skyline of peaked slate roofs and ironwork spires. After a few moments more the hospital disappeared from her sight completely, disarming the sky.